THE
ONE•SHOT
WAR

THE ONE·SHOT WAR

a novel by

BRIAN O'CONNOR

Times
BOOKS

Published by TIMES BOOKS, a division of
Quadrangle/The New York Times Book Co., Inc.
Three Park Avenue, New York, NY 10016

Published simultaneously in Canada by
Fitzhenry & Whiteside, Ltd., Toronto.

Copyright © 1980 by Brian O'Connor.

All rights reserved. No part of this book may
be reproduced in any form or by any electronic
or mechanical means including information storage
and retrieval systems without permission in writing
from the publisher, except by a reviewer who may
quote brief passages in a review.

Library of Congress Cataloging in Publication Data

O'Connor, Brian.
The one-shot war.
I. Title.
PR6065.C5305 1980   823'.914   80-5147
ISBN 0-8129-0939-9

MANUFACTURED IN THE UNITED STATES OF AMERICA.

THE
ONE·SHOT
WAR

• ONE •

THE MAN CALMLY PUFFED the small cigar and waited. At last it was to begin.

He glanced at the wooden-cased mantelpiece clock, forgetting momentarily that it had ceased to function a long time ago. Checking his watch, he saw that the first arrival was due in ten minutes. The little strategem of staged arrivals had probably never made the slightest difference, but they all seemed to expect it.

He had conceived the plan six months previously. The small newspaper article had planted the seed, subsequent events had nurtured it, and now, at last, it was to come to fruition.

Of course the opposition would be tremendous. The others were essentially small-scale men, content to sit back and let events carry them along. Some of them were just dead weight carried by previous deeds and reputations, but now obsolete. An undertaking of this magnitude was sure to intimidate them. . . .

The terraced Dublin house was in a quiet street off the North Circular Road, just two minutes walk from the main Phoenix Park gates. The first man arrived on schedule, followed by the others at five minute intervals, until there were six in all. They greeted each other with the familiarity born out of numerous other such meetings. Although it was a mild night, a bright coal fire reddened the grate. They spent a few minutes in idle talk before the Leader called the meeting to order, then each took his usual place around the mahogany table and waited.

The Leader looked at their expectant faces. He would bring them along slowly, giving them just enough to sway them.

"Gentlemen, you are probably wondering why I have called together this extraordinary meeting of the Army Council."

Just like a company director, he thought. The analogy made him smile slightly. First, a sharp reminder to soften them up.

"As you know, we've lost more men and arms in the past six months than in the previous five years. With the security situation at present, we're finding it difficult to even move our materials around, let alone mount active operations."

"We're getting enough through, and morale is still very high," interjected Peadar O'Murchu, a truculent bushy-haired man in his mid-fifties. In numerous British Army bases his photograph appeared above the anglicized version of his name—Peter Murphy—a fact that enraged him. He was their Quartermaster-General in Belfast, responsible for the collection and distribution of all arms and explosives used in that city. He was quick to take offense, and had to be dealt with somewhat diplomatically.

The Leader looked directly at him. Flattery was the man's weak point.

"Peadar, under the circumstances, what you've been achieving up there has been tremendous."

O'Murchu was somewhat mollified.

"However," continued the Leader quickly, "we must remind ourselves again of the enormous difficulties we are now facing."

Dick Power, a small stockily built man, commented mildly, "The American connection has opened up again." He was their liaison with fund-raising groups abroad.

"It would want to," said O'Murchu bitterly. "Jesus, if we had all the help that they promised us, we'd have beaten the British years ago. Yanks, they're all piss and wind!"

"Don't talk rubbish," Power admonished him. "They spend months collecting nickels and dimes. Finally, they have enough to buy a case-load of rifles and ship them over, and what happens? One of our men is driving up north with the guns, an army patrol stops him, and that's the end of that shipment. All for nothing. It disheartens them."

"Look," said O'Murchu, his temper rising, "I've got sixteen and seventeen year olds shooting at reinforced armored cars with old Lee-Enfields that nobody else would touch, so don't talk to me about how disheartened those slobs in the States are."

"That's enough," the Leader cut in. "Let's stop arguing amongst ourselves. I've called this extraordinary meeting to gain your approval for something that will end the war within a short time."

That'll quieten them, he thought. Gain their approval... Events had been set in motion long before and there was no turning back. There must be no leaks.

Five faces looked expectantly at him.

"In the last few years," he commenced, "there has been a dramatic change of events in these islands. Charles Douglas has been British Prime Minister for most of those years. The conclusion is obvious."

"That bastard!" said one of the men venomously. "He looks on himself as another bloody Churchill."

The Leader acknowledged the comment with a nod.

"He certainly talks enough about his so-called destiny. But in his case it's not just talk. He really believes it. No matter what we may think of him, there's no denying the enormous changes he's brought about in Britain. Strikes virtually eliminated, the economy booming; it's a pretty impressive achievement in such a short time. With the greatly increased standards of living it's not surprising that he's got very broad support at present."

One or two of the men shifted impatiently in their seats. They weren't here for a history lesson.

The Leader noticed their impatience but continued speaking in his usual measured tones. "However, Douglas' support, though broad, is also shallow. To achieve his success he has, of necessity, had to alienate many different groups. There is a growing feeling of concern over there at the curtailments of freedom that have developed since he took office. Unfortunately, with a General Election due next year, it seems virtually certain that he and his party will be re-elected. And that, gentlemen, from our point of view, is very bad news, indeed."

"We've survived for a long time up to now," said O'Murchu with the unshakable certainty of the zealot. "We won't be beaten by Douglas or by anybody else."

"Agreed," said the Leader. "We can survive, despite our present difficulties. Undoubtedly we have the capacity to tie down the enemy for a long time to come." He paused to relight his cigar. "However, survival in itself is no great cause for celebration. As things stand they're the elephant and we're the flea on its back. It's a stalemate. . . ."

"So, what's this suggestion of yours?" asked O'Murchu.

The Leader spread his hands. "Since Douglas became Prime Minister, our cause has regained some of its support abroad, particularly in America. I say regained because, as you all know, this support was totally estranged by previous bombing incidents."

Everybody except the Leader glanced at another man who stared coldly into space. He was the previous Chief of Staff and it was under him that most of the bombings had occurred. It was the backlash to these that had in turn led to him being replaced as the Leader. His name was Brendan Coffey. Feeling that he was expected to say something, Coffey commented sourly.

"All the foreign pressure in the world won't effect that man Douglas."

"Exactly," said the Leader. "Douglas is the key and that's why we're meeting here tonight. In exactly two weeks time the Prime Minister is going to America. Our decision is whether or not he will ever return. . . ."

The flat statement took the men by surprise. They had all planned numerous operations and were no strangers to sudden death, but the assassination of a British Prime Minister in office was enough to startle even the most hardened of them. A Minister might be possible, but the Prime Minister himself? They had, of course, used assassination as a political weapon in the past. However, despite the enormous publicity that these killings had generated, the resultant massive security clampdowns and widespread foreign condemnation had been sobering.

A buzz of conversation swept the room.

Let them gabble, thought the Leader. It had to seem like they were making the decision. He could almost see the way the vote was splitting. Two in favor, two against, and one, quiet, pipe-smoking Niall Kelly, still uncommitted.

Finally, Dick Power almost whispered, "How could it be done?"

"I have a proposal which we can consider, once we have agreed to the action in principle. Most important of all, we must calculate the effect of such an assassination. Just think, gentlemen. Removing

Douglas will lead to a situation somewhat similar to what it was before he came to power. It will leave a vacuum in which we will be in a far stronger position than we were then."

"It seems like he's been there forever," commented Power wearily.

The impact of Douglas' premiership was such that it had completely overshadowed that of his immediate predecessor who, several years earlier, had tried to end the deadlock in Northern Ireland. After a long and tortuous period of alternately stonewalling and sounding out all the interested parties at home and abroad, and after one previous inconclusive attempt, the then Prime Minister had finally decided that the intolerable situation must be tackled with firm and decisive action. A whole generation had already grown up since the cauldron of political and religious violence had first exploded, and still the problem remained unresolved. In a new initiative, Douglas' predecessor had tried to break out of the historical straightjacket in which each of the participants was hopelessly imprisoned. Public opinion in Britain would no longer tolerate a seemingly endless conflict. It was clear that in the absence of a negotiated settlement, the British link with the Province could not be indefinitely guaranteed.

The Prime Minister's approach to the problem received a mixed reception. In Britain itself, it was generally welcomed despite the opposition of those politicians who regarded any talk of a British withdrawal as a concession to terrorism and an unacceptable volte-face. In their view it was unthinkable that a British government would even consider such an action. Charles Douglas was a senior Cabinet Minister at the time. He was one of those who argued strongly against the proposals but always confined his criticism to Inner Cabinet meetings. The criticism was blunted by the Prime Minister's unshakable determination to create an atmosphere conducive to progress.

After a short period, the initiative was eventually as dead as the Prime Minister who instigated it. A massive brain hemorrhage had struck with chilling finality.

The new Prime Minister was chosen by the Parliamentary Party. After four days deliberation it was Charles Douglas who drove to

Buckingham Palace to see the Queen.

In his first week in office, Douglas publicly clarified his position on the threat of any possible British withdrawal from the Province. While fully recognizing the desirability of political progress, such a step was simply out of the question under any circumstances. The primary task of his administration would be the defeat of terrorism and the restoration of law and order. Security operations would be effectively stepped up to achieve this aim.

The Leader's voice was very soft now. "It certainly does seem as if he's been there forever. You remember the criticism he received at the time for not persisting with that initiative. There's still a strong feeling amongst British politicians, particularly in the Opposition Parties, that the Irish question should have been settled once and for all. By removing Douglas we will allow this feeling to be given expression in more concrete terms."

"I wouldn't count on it," interrupted Brendan Coffey, the former Chief of Staff. "In my view assassinating their Prime Minister could set us back years. Even if we were successful, which I very much doubt, the consequences are too unpredictable. . . ."

The Leader controlled his irritation. As usual, Coffey would oppose him at every opportunity. He had never concealed his resentment at losing the leadership. "That's not the way I see it, Brendan. At first, of course, the British will close ranks tightly against us. There will be condemnation from all sides and a widespread increase in army activities. They'll push us so hard that we won't be able to put our noses outside the door. And we won't. Just token resistance to let them know that the flea is still in business." He smiled sardonically. "But I estimate that after the initial crackdown they'll start to ease off. The big changes will come later. Most important of all there will be enormous political changes in Britain. The Opposition Parties there will concentrate on the less savory aspects of Douglas' premiership. This, coupled with the virtual emasculation of his party without him, could ensure a change of government shortly. I think that by then there is a reasonable chance they will seek to withdraw."

"But no guarantee," someone muttered.

The Leader looked at the man and smiled. "There are never guarantees, just reasonable assumptions. What can they do? In a year we will have used the time underground to rearm and retrain our units. The new government has either the choice of years of conflict or a clean break. I think that, after a decent interval, they'll go for a break."

"You've sprung this on us fairly suddenly," said O'Murchu sharply. "It's not something that we should have to make a snap decision on. What's the hurry? Why not wait till Douglas comes back from America?"

The Leader knew he was on dangerous ground. He spoke quietly, convincingly. "Peadar, this is something that I've thought about for some time. I didn't want to bring it up until I had a definite proposal to put before you. We have an opportunity here which we simply must not waste. It allows us to exploit the fact that Douglas will be on strange ground and vulnerable, in a country where we have a considerable organization. The situation in London is just too tight for us at present. Douglas has confined his public appearances to a bare minimum and never moves without a posse of armed security personnel, all marksmen." His voice grew more forceful. "Circumstances will never be better for us than they are now. If we act boldly we can accomplish our objectives with this one single blow."

"I take it you have someone in mind for the job?" asked Niall Kelly. This was his first contribution to the meeting.

The Leader nodded. "That Crossmaglen boy, Jim Duffy. He's a good shot, he's been in action a lot, and he can take orders. He's under your section, Niall. What do you think of him?"

Kelly considered. "Well, he's an excellent shot, no doubt about that. He's had three hits since he went active. But that's a long way from assassinating a figure like Douglas." He sucked contemplatively on his pipe. "I'll say this, he's totally dedicated to the Movement and would certainly give it his best. If you can get him within a hundred yards of the Prime Minister with a rifle, I think he's got the nerve."

He leaned back as if this homily had exhausted him.

About as much chance of doing that as getting him to Mars, thought the Leader.

"Yes, that should be possible," he said aloud. "The point is, if we get him into position we want someone who is capable of doing the job. I think Duffy could be the man to handle it."

Brendan Coffey's voice was skeptical. "You do realize that even if by some miracle he succeeded, the chances of him getting out alive are virtually nil. At best he probably faces a lifetime in an American prison. At best."

The Leader looked at his predecessor coolly. "I know you are concerned for all our volunteers, Brendan, but Duffy will of course be given the alternative of refusing."

"He won't refuse," cut in Kelly with contempt, as if the thought of one of his men refusing a direct Army Council request was unthinkable. "He's lost one brother and two cousins to date. For a chance of a crack at Douglas, he'd swim to America."

"If he's that keen," said Coffey acidly, "why not give him a gun and let him go right up to the Prime Minister and shoot him from five feet?"

"Because nobody unscreened will get within fifty yards of Douglas," said the Leader. "Duffy might just get one shot off before they stopped him. That's if, by some chance, he got close enough to use a handgun. No, I'm not sending him on a suicide mission, even if he agreed."

Though I would if I felt it would work, he thought to himself.

"No, to penetrate the security it's got to be a long-distance affair. If we use Duffy, we'll get him in position and do our best to get him out again. Which brings me to the actual method."

Briefly he paused, and then spoke for three more minutes. When he had finished he sat down.

Dick Power whistled. "Jesus, it's so hare-brained it might just work," he said admiringly.

Two of the others nodded. It was so outrageous that it might, just might do. Two remained unimpressed.

Yes, he had them now. The idea had gripped them and they were getting enthusiastic. Time to push hard.

"Gentlemen, I propose that we conclude this matter without further delay. Let us now vote on it."

Nice and democratic.

"Those in favor?"

Three hands rose up.

"Those against?"

Two hands this time.

He didn't vote himself, glad he didn't have to use his deciding vote.

The men waited for another half an hour, discussing various aspects of the plan. Then they started to leave singly, as they had come. The last to leave was the former Chief of Staff. He had been one of those to vote against the plan. Brendan Coffey looked intently at the Leader as he spoke.

"You know what will happen if this cocks up, as it almost certainly will? If we try to hit Douglas and fail, we'll be squeezed so tight that it might destroy us completely."

"I've considered that. It's worth the risk," the Leader replied evenly.

His predecessor gave him a puzzled look and then slipped out.

He suspects something all right, thought the Leader.

He sat down and lit another small cigar. After a minute he poured a small Jameson and waited, humming tunelessly to himself.

As the last man left the house a figure detached itself from the shadows of a small passageway, a hundred yards up the road. Five in, five out, he thought to himself.

Still Kevin Dalton didn't move. He stayed completely motionless for another half an hour. He had been in the same position for two hours, but if he was weary he didn't show it.

Satisfied, he finally moved unhurriedly down the road to the house. He opened the door and entered.

The Leader tapped his cigar ash into the dying fire.

"Come in Kevin," he said. "Pour a whiskey and sit down. We have much to talk about."

"They went for it?" the new arrival asked. It was more a statement than a question.

"Easier than I thought," said the Leader. "I expected Kelly might be sticky, but the idea of a Crossmaglen boy doing the job swung him. With the publicity they've had, they think it's cowboy country up there and they're all Jesse James."

Dalton smiled. The man facing him was one of the few men whom he really liked—a liking born of respect.

"Do you have everything ready for me?" he inquired, knowing the answer.

The Leader looked mock-pained. "Wait here. I'll be down in a minute."

When he returned he gave the younger man a bulky package. "Check them all," he said.

Five minutes later, Dalton raised his head. "Looks perfect."

"Ought to be," said the Leader, "they're the real thing."

"Any chance of them being traced?"

"Not for a long time and even if they did, it would just be a blind alley."

"Who fixed them up—Brady?"

"Yes. He also arranged the visa and other documentation you wanted. They're all in order."

"There'll be no problem with him I suppose?" Dalton asked pointedly.

The Leader looked straight into his eyes.

"Two nights ago Brady was shot dead in Belfast. The police reckon it was another sectarian killing."

Dalton shoved the package deep into his parka pocket. It was necessary. The human side of him felt regret, but he pushed it to the back of his mind. He was always professional about it and had to continue that way. The stakes were too high for sentiment.

"Let's go over it again," said the Leader brusquely.

One hour later Dalton stood up.

"Good luck and God bless," said the older man. He spoke with finality, his eyes shiny with emotion.

Strange, thought Dalton, he's usually so self-contained.

Silently he slipped out the door.

• TWO •

THE 747 CIRCLED over Kennedy Airport. It had been waiting for landing clearance for just over one hour. To the pilot and cabin crew, it was just another normal flight hiccup; to the passengers, many of them first-time tourists keyed up over their introductory glimpse of America, it was slightly deflating. Their departure from Gatwick had already been delayed by three hours due to the domino effect of a strike by French air traffic controllers.

In the mid-section center aisle, a lightly tanned and casually dressed man appeared to be asleep. Only when the captain announced their final descent did he open his eyes. Stretching his legs gratefully, he sat up.

He was of medium height and slim build. A large shock of light-brown hair complemented his beard and mustache. His passport named him as Robert Dickenson, thirty-one years of age, a British citizen resident in Brighton, and an art teacher by profession.

Kevin Dalton closed the passport. He felt quite relaxed, but with just the right degree of tautness to keep him alert. He looked at his tanned forearms and smiled. Ten days under the hot Spanish sun had given his normally pale skin just enough tan. He would fit in without too much trouble. A small detail, but they were the ones that could kill you.

He glanced again at the passport. The details fit him well enough. They could have fit thousands of men. His photograph stared back at him. The only difference between his passport and any other was that the photograph on it was different from the supposedly corresponding photograph on record at the passport office in London. There might have been an outside chance of them making some connection, but he didn't want to present them with his photograph. Not now. Not after all these years.

Forty-five minutes later he had passed through immigration control. The officer had deftly checked his visa against the list, found the name, and allowed him through with a mechanical, "Welcome to the United States."

In the terminal, he removed his Laker luggage stickers and replaced them with a Pan Am tag.

Outside the terminal he hailed a cab.

Even though he had just arrived, he felt that surge of exhilaration which New York seemed to give its visitors. The cab reached midtown Manhattan forty minutes later and pulled up at a hotel on East Forty-fourth Street.

The hotel had a large, busy lobby. The stairs were situated just to the left of the reception area, with the elevators to the right. Dalton knew that he could pass in and out of the hotel with relative ease, without being noticed. He checked in and paid for a week in advance. A fully paid bill tends to decrease interest in a hotel resident's comings and goings. He answered all the clerk's queries in an American accent, and minutes later was closing the door on the bald fifty-year-old bellboy, who departed reasonably happy with his dollar tip.

Two minutes later he left the hotel. He found a public phone and dialed a number in the Bronx.

"Hello, Dominic Lynch speaking," said the voice on the other end, the soft Kerry accent overlaid with a harsher New York rasp.

"Do you know who this is?" asked Dalton brusquely.

"I've been expecting your call for the last four hours," said Lynch matter-of-factly.

"I just want you to listen," Dalton cut in. "Then repeat what I tell you. Nothing else. Understood?"

"Yes."

He spoke rapidly and clearly for three more minutes. "Now repeat it," he ordered.

Lynch complied. Immediately after he had finished, the phone clicked dead in his hands.

"Sociable bastard," he muttered to himself, replacing the receiver. Still, he liked the directness of the man.

As Dalton walked back to his hotel he felt comfortably tired. Tomorrow would be a long day and he wanted to be fresh and alert. He believed in being in good physical shape. A tired body makes a tired mind and a tired mind makes stupid mistakes. He always tried to eliminate these mistakes. Most times they could be eliminated by taking the obvious precautions. The cardinal rule was never to assume anything. Basically, survival was a matter of superior planning. The constant double-checking that this entailed often wasted time and was eventually irrelevant. The occasional time that it wasn't was what kept you alive. By always following his rules, he had outlived many others. . . .

At the entrance to his hotel he stopped and inhaled deeply. An earlier cloudburst had freshened the air. After a few seconds he turned and entered the lobby. Before going up to his room, he left instructions with the reception clerk to call him the next morning at seven-thirty A.M.

Once in his room he opened the window as wide as possible. Luckily, the temperature wasn't unduly high for that time in summer. He could do without the irritating hum of the air conditioner. He undressed, unbuckled the thick money belt from around his waist, and carefully placed it under the pillow.

As he lay in his shorts on the bed, the sounds and smells of the city touched his senses, though not unpleasantly. He thought of his first introduction to New York. So many years ago. At that time he had obtained a temporary work permit, available to foreign students to work in the United States. He had worked in a fast-food restaurant and spent his spare time exploring the city. Its reputation for violence was daunting, but he watched what areas he went to and behaved sensibly. Still, even then and on subsequent visits, he could never quite shake that feeling of slight danger which the city generated. Most other large American cities gave him that same feeling.

In the fast-food restaurant he had a pleasant manner and was always efficient and strictly honest. At the end of his temporary working period he returned to Ireland and his studies. At that stage he was unaware of the changes that were about to occur in his life.

The civil rights marches in Derry had given way to a seemingly irreversible process of violence.

Dalton slept.

• THREE •

HE WAS BACK on the hill again. The sky was just turning dark, and the army patrol was threading its way along the small unapproved road. His four-man active-service unit was three hundred yards from the Irish Republic border, but inside Northern Ireland and, therefore, still on British soil.

He could just hear the patrol. The soft scrape of a hob-nailed boot on the road as the soldiers crisscrossed from side to side. He could visualize the instructor warning them—always move in an irregular fashion; never walk straight, makes you a sitting target; cover one another, last man facing backward.

Dalton pulled on the thin surgical gloves, slipped a rag out of his parka, and carefully wiped the gun down. He looked at the young man on his left. Even in the fading light he could see the pale face, rigid with fear. Sean Kerrigan was eighteen. Dalton had joined at about the same time. Dalton gave him a tight smile but doubted if the fellow even saw him.

On Dalton's right were two other men. The nearest one, Paul Dempsey, seemed okay, but the fingers gripping the butt of his Thompson were bone-white. On the far right was Frank Glass, large and mustached.

Glass was the senior member of the group. He was in command of the three rookies to his left, but he didn't know how they would react. Two looked okay, but the last one on the left looked frozen. It happened sometimes when the reality of the situation hit them.

The one next to him, that guy Dalton, he couldn't figure out. Too bloody quiet for his liking. Never said an unnecessary word. Pleasant enough, but very self-contained. The way he pulled on those gloves was typical. Fair enough, he took the occasional drink or two after a meeting, but was nearly always first to leave. Wasn't very popular with the others, but didn't seem to care. To give him credit, he was good in training. Picked up things quickly and didn't forget them. Whereas many of the others looked on the pre-operational training as a bore, he took it very seriously; when it came to stripping a rifle down blindfolded and reassembling it, he did it smoother and quicker than any of them. Even himself, Glass admitted ruefully.

When they finally got down to the quiet mountain training site in Cork, he wondered how the fellow would react to actually firing a gun. He needn't have worried. After two hours of practice he had to concede that the man was a first-class shot—a marksman if ever he'd seen one.

After a number of such training sessions they were ready to go in at short notice. Two weeks later they got the word. They traveled by car to Dundalk, switched cars there, and picked up the guns at a safe house just on the Irish side of the border. Half an hour later they were over the border and in position.

Back at the farmhouse, Glass had noticed Dalton glancing at a small map. Planning his way out again if anything happens to me, he had surmised. Absolutely right, of course, but Glass had felt as if someone were walking over his grave.

They were very close now. Dalton heard a muted voice whisper something. He didn't know what regiment they were. Not that it mattered. It was dark now but with enough moonlight to make the countryside clearly visible. He watched the bend in the road and saw the first figure come into view. Slowly the others followed, single-file, moving irregularly.

He looked at Glass, who had warned them not to fire until he fired first. The patrol moved sharply along the road until eight soldiers were visible. Dalton sighted on the head of the fourth man. He guessed, correctly, that the others would shoot for the front of the column.

When the first soldier was only thirty yards away Dalton heard a loud crack to his right and saw the soldier crumple, clutching his leg.

He squeezed the trigger of his own weapon and saw his target collapse to the ground. He was sighting on another target when the rattle of Dempsey's Thompson filled the night. It was way off target.

There was no sound from his left.

The patrol members were trained, professional soldiers and didn't waste any time in seeking cover. They couldn't see where their ambushers were, but raked the general direction of the flashes with sustained light-machine-gun fire.

The firing continued for ten minutes. As it went on, the patrol identified the area where their assailants were, and their fire became more steady and accurate.

Suddenly Paul Dempsey slipped backward, blood spurting from his throat.

Dalton could feel the gun becoming uncomfortably hot in his hands, but kept systematically spreading his bullets around.

Useless. Bloody useless. It was just pure luck now. That was what he hated most of all—it was out of his control.

Glass turned to him and hissed, "Let's get the fuck out." As he moved to get up, his head disintegrated and he rolled gently down the hill.

Dalton looked to his left. The young lad, Sean, was totally rigid. His eyes were wide open and staring straight ahead. He was trying to say something—a prayer?—but all that came out was a strangled gargle. Dalton gripped his arm and urgently spat, "Come on Sean, it's time to go."

He looked down the incline and saw a figure charging up the hill. The clay was flaking up around him as the soldiers' covering fire bit deep into the earth. Dalton sighted calmly on the nearing figure and gently squeezed the trigger.

Nothing happened.

Seized up, he thought disgustedly. Too bloody old.

The soldier was only about fifteen yards away. Dalton could clearly see the three stripes on his arm. He dropped the rifle, grabbed Sean's gun, and simultaneously kicked the boy in the chest to send him sprawling down the safe side of the hill.

The soldier was practically on him as Dalton stood up and hip-shot him. The sergeant took it full in the chest and rolled backward. Now Dalton could see the other figures moving up after him.

He fired two aimless rounds, turned, and dived down the hill. Sean was kneeling there.

". . . who art in heaven, hallowed be thy name," he could hear him croaking.

Dalton pulled him to his feet and half dragged him along. Sean responded to the urgency and started to run. As they crashed through the undergrowth, the boy was still mumbling.

"Thy kingdom come, Thy will be done on earth . . ."

The soldier's passed their dead sergeant's body.

Two hundred yards to the border. That's if they don't cross over after us, thought Dalton. With at least two of their men dead, he wouldn't want to bet against it.

" . . . as it is in Heaven."

The gunfire exploded behind them as the soldiers charged over the crest of the hill. Dalton veered right through a gap in the hedge, guiding Sean by the arm. Someone must have heard Sean's prayers as just then the moon disappeared temporarily behind a cloud. They raced through the small field on the other side of the hedge, oblivious to any hidden obstacles.

The soldiers were firing blindly at their backs, guessing their whereabouts from their noisy progress.

The sounds of pursuit continued for about another minute, and then abruptly ceased. Dalton kept going for nearly another four hundred yards until his lungs were bursting. Only then did he collapse to the ground.

He lay there recovering for a full three minutes.

Slowly his heart stopped pounding and his breathing returned to normal. Looking down, he noticed that he was still holding the rifle. He laid it on the ground, peeled off the gloves, and replaced them in his parka.

He wasn't exactly sure where they were, but it couldn't be too far from the farmhouse where they had left the car. He brought the docile Sean along, clutching his arm by the sleeve, and twenty minutes later they turned into the farmhouse.

The old man who let them in looked questioningly at them. Dalton ignored him. He went into the toilet and carefully wiped down the rifle before returning it to the farmer. What happened to it after that was not his business.

Ten minutes later he was driving toward Dundalk with Sean by his side. The boy was staring fixedly ahead, still obviously in shock. Dalton glanced at him briefly and then tried to empty the anger from his mind.

In Dundalk he left Sean in a house, switched cars, and set out back to Dublin. When he arrived, he went directly to a house in Sandymount. He was ushered into the front room and was joined there by another man a few seconds later.

"Well, what happened?" the man asked brusquely.

Dalton's scornful face and the fact that he was alone told him that something was badly wrong.

"Screw-up total and complete," said Dalton disgustedly. "If we keep going like that we might as well forget about it. We had the advantage of surprise. We picked the time and place of ambush and what happened? We got two soldiers. That's it! If we were any good we should have got the whole bloody lot of them."

The man looked stonily at him.

Dalton shook his head bitterly. "We've got two dead, one a mental cripple, and three lost weapons out of the four we had!"

"Who got the soldiers?" the man asked him.

Dalton told him.

The man nodded. "Go on."

"There's nothing to go on about."

"Still I'd like to hear everything," the man said evenly.

Dalton looked at him sharply and then briefly related the whole episode.

The other's face grew sorrowful as he heard of Glass's death. "A good man, hard to replace," he murmured.

When Dalton had finished his report, the man lit a small cigar and inhaled deeply. Before speaking, he looked reflectively at Dalton for a few seconds.

"You did well. Go home now and get some sleep."

That night remained vivid in his memories. He had come under fire, and it held no terrors. He could recall every minute of the night's events and knew that he was thinking clearly all the time. When his own life was in danger, he had reacted with the maximum efficiency.

In the following months and years, he accepted this ability as a part of himself and used it accordingly. He knew that he could dispassionately consider his own death and not allow that possibility to inhibit his judgment.

His background was unremarkable. His father, a teacher, was

fluent in Irish, and sported a small gold Fainne—a ring worn on the lapel to indicate that he spoke Irish and would prefer to converse in that tongue. His mother was also a teacher, her father having been active in the old troubles. Her family home had been strongly Republican. Kevin's grandfather had come to live with them for some years before his death and had often talked to the young boy about those long-gone days.

An only child, Kevin had come to his parents when they had almost reconciled themselves to being childless. He had grown up in a close-knit, nationalist-minded family, and from an early age had always been self-contained and self-reliant. Though outwardly courteous and pleasant, he was content with his own company and did not willingly seek the friendship of others. He decided to study architecture and seemed set for a promising career.

When he came back from America he had returned to his studies untroubled. Then his father died suddenly, and his mother followed shortly afterward.

With the loss of his parents, the center of his world collapsed. His solitary nature prevented him from sharing his grief, and, if anything, time magnified rather than diminished his sense of isolation. Events were shaping up around him, and he found himself becoming increasingly involved. Nurtured by his family tradition, his involvement formed a focal point for his grief at that time. The final factor that edged him into violence was Bloody Sunday in Derry.

The conflict was escalating. . . .

In the next year Dalton went on seven more missions. The casualty rate amongst his associates was high due to inefficiency and loose planning rather than any lack of enthusiasm. As he grew more experienced, Dalton began to assume more responsibility for his own safety.

Two days after his seventh mission, he was unexpectedly summoned to the small house in Sandymount to which he had reported after his first mission. Again he met the same man as on that night. The man was alone. He handed Dalton a whiskey.

"Sit down, Kevin, I want to have a talk with you."

The man asked him a few questions, listening attentively to his replies. He then spoke nonstop for almost fifteen minutes. He told

Dalton that he had received first-class reports on him from a number of sources. He had followed his career with interest since the first night they had met. He had been looking for someone like Dalton for a long time. He anticipated a long, drawn-out struggle and wanted someone to work directly for him in a special capacity.

He suggested that Dalton drop out of the Movement completely. He would explain it to the other members, and had enough influence to insure that it was accepted without protest.

From that day on Dalton would go underground. He would be responsible only to the man and take all orders from him. Any information that the Movement had on him would be destroyed.

He would be called on irregularly to carry out specific jobs when the Movement most needed results and security was too tight for normal action. The man would arrange weapon delivery and collection, and would provide all the necessary information. Dalton would plan and carry out the jobs completely on his own.

After the man had finished, Dalton sat silently. The prospect of working alone appealed to him from both a practical and a personal viewpoint. Despite his precautions he knew that it was only a matter of time before he paid for someone else's mistake. For too long now his life had depended on the inefficiency of others. . . .

Time passed and the conflict dragged on. Only a few top people in the Movement knew about Dalton. Even then they didn't know the full story. The only man who could tell them eventually became Leader.

Kevin Dalton became an expert in the one-shot war.

• FOUR •

THE STRIDENT RING of the telephone cut through his sleep. "Your seven-thirty call, sir," the voice told him.

Dalton rose immediately and quickly showered and dressed. Minutes later he was leaving the hotel.

He breakfasted in a coffee shop just up the street, and later walked over to the Vanderbilt Avenue entrance of Grand Central Station. Once inside, he went down the stairs to the Main Concourse and bought a copy of *The New York Times*. Returning up the stairs, he leaned against the marble balustrade and opened his paper. This site offered a commanding view of the main station but was screened from the locker area under the staircase.

Ten minutes later, a well-built young man with a slightly receding hairline entered the other end of the station. He was carrying three identical carry-alls with leather grips. Danny Moore walked confidently up the station to the left luggage lockers and selected a couple of large lockers. Two of the carry-alls he put into one locker. The third, bulkier one went into a separate locker of its own. He locked them in and dropped the keys into a brown envelope. After a brief glance around, Moore crossed the station to the waiting area just off the Main Concourse. Here he purchased a copy of the *Daily News* and sat down on one of the benches. He opened the paper and started to read.

Dalton had watched him crossing the station. He quickly walked down the marble staircase and over to the Off-Track Betting cage near the waiting area. While deliberating over his betting ticket, he could see through the wire cage into the waiting area.

One minute later, Danny Moore folded his paper and stood up. As he walked back into the Main Concourse, he dropped the paper onto one of the metal garbage bins near the OTB cage. He then turned right and headed toward the Lexington Avenue entrance without looking back.

Dalton was coming out of the OTB cage as Moore turned the corner. After a few steps he halted beside the waste can, glanced at his betting ticket, and then abruptly crumpled it into the trash. Apparently noticing the newspaper, he picked it up as if checking the date. Confident that Moore would be out of sight by now, he continued on into the station.

As he moved unhurriedly toward the lockers, he could feel the hard outline of the keys taped inside the paper. He removed the three carry-alls from their resting places and quickly left the station.

Outside, he caught a cab and headed across town to Penn Station. Deep in its locker area he opened the carry-alls, briefly checked their contents, and then placed them in three separate lockers. Satisfied, he pocketed the keys and left.

Once again, Dalton hailed a cab.

This deposited him at a large midtown car rental agency. He produced a license, which was duly scrutinized by one of the clerks. The license identified him as Alan Green, with an address in Queens. He paid cash and shortly afterward was heading downtown to Greenwich Village in his rented car.

Traffic was heavy and the journey took longer than he wanted.

Once in the Village he left the car near Washington Square, and a brisk ten-minute walk brought him to his destination.

He entered a well-stocked electrical goods shop, explained his requests to the assistant, and left shortly afterward with his purchases.

After a quick lunch in a nearby delicatessen, he found a pay phone and dialed a Manhattan number. The voice at the other end was pleasantly accommodating.

"Yes, that can be easily arranged," he was told.

"And I would definitely like someone who is used to children, preferably a parent himself. My young son will be accompanying me, and he's a bit nervous."

"No problem," said the voice, taking the bait easily. "Resinelli has a couple of his own."

"But is he an experienced man?" asked Dalton anxiously. "I don't want someone who's just learning the ropes."

"Very experienced. He's been doing it practically every day for five years now," the anonymous voice reassured him.

"Okay. I'll be down later to pay in advance, and you can tell this Resinelli that there'll be a real good tip for him if everything goes well. Will I be able to speak to him today?"

"If you're down before five o'clock. He'll be leaving then."

"Thank you. I'll be there."

Dalton replaced the receiver and returned to his car.

Shortly afterward he arrived at Battery Park. He was at the southern tip of the island of Manhattan, looking out over the harbor that holds one of the most familiar sights in the world.

The Statue of Liberty. With her torch held sternly upward to the sky, she drew the eyes of the crowd on the jetty like a magnet.

He took out a small but powerful pair of binoculars and focused them on the statue. He could easily make out the tiny figures moving around in the crown.

The next ferry out was due to depart in fifteen minutes.

He queued patiently at the ticket office, purchased his ticket, and joined the other people streaming onto the ferry. Shortly afterward the crew pulled up the ramps and the ferry started the short trip out to the statue. As it moved farther from the shore it offered a panoramic view of the New York skyline. The World Trade Center dominated the other skyscrapers.

The ferry was packed with excited tourists. The sun was streaming down, and everybody was happy. The children licked their ice cream cones, and their parents looked on approvingly. Was not this what America was all about? Many of the parents were themselves immigrants or first-generation Americans and today they were visiting one of the greatest symbols of freedom in the world.

The ferry gently bumped into position, and the passengers disembarked. Most of them hurried inside the statue to study its secrets. Dalton walked around the perimeter of the small island on which the statue was situated, occasionally glancing outward. When he had completed his inspection he returned to the entrance.

He passed inside the museum and moved among the throngs of people gazing at the various exhibits. These recalled the history of the United States, the arrival of the different waves of immigrants, and their effect on the creation and molding of America.

In one section, a series of tape recordings echoed what some of the signers of the Declaration of Independence might have said at the time. He noticed that a few of them were Irish. Their "taped" voices had authentic Irish accents, though they were Southern Irish accents, not the very distinct Scots-Irish twang of Ulster. The irony of it appealed to him. Most of the Irish members of the independence movement in revolutionary America were, in fact, Ulster Protestants who had left their native country disenchanted with English rule. Only seventy years later did the "true" Irish arrive, fleeing from the Great Famine.

He moved on. In another section was a display of lifelike figures, clothed in the period dress worn by the different immigrant groups. Swedes and Germans, Irish, English, and Dutch, all in their best traveling clothes; some well-dressed and prosperous, others markedly less so.

He looked at the two Irish figures, clothed in their old rags. They looked what they were: poor and illiterate peasants, oppressed and hungry, having to leave their own soil forever. To his surprise he found himself oddly touched, even a little angry. He welcomed the sensation, strangely relieved that he could still feel such simple emotion.

"The ferry will be departing in approximately fifteen minutes," announced the metallic voice, breaking into his thoughts. He quickly concentrated his mind and moved along toward the exit.

Five minutes later he reboarded the ferry for the return journey. As it pulled away he glanced around once more at the statue and, for a few brief seconds, remembered the strange emotion he had felt a little earlier. He then firmly fixed his sights on the approaching Manhattan shore. . . .

It was just after four o'clock when he arrived at his next destination. He pulled into a parking lot seventy yards up from a long, prefabricated building; he was near enough to keep it in view, yet still far enough away to be missed by a casual observer from the building.

Before leaving the car, he put a peaked corduroy cap on his head. The cap was tight-fitting, with a band of soft elastic on its inner rim, and it covered his large shock of hair.

He got out and walked down toward the building. A few cars were parked on the blacktop outside. He went inside, approached the counter, and asked for Mr. Resinelli.

"Just missed him. Should be back in about twenty-five minutes," a fair-haired man informed him.

Dalton sat down and waited. A number of other people were present, one or two looking slightly apprehensive. The time passed slowly.

Finally a door opened behind the counter and a man entered. He looked about forty, with thick, wind-swept hair and a large figure running to fat. The man spoke to his fair-haired colleague who then nodded in Dalton's direction.

The new arrival signaled toward Dalton, and Dalton went up to the counter and shook hands.

"Mr. Resinelli, I presume?" he inquired pleasantly.

"Just call me Angelo," the man said in a friendly tone.

Dalton quickly repeated his previous phoned request and Resinelli nodded in agreement.

"Sure, no sweat," he said.

"You're quite certain that the boy will be okay?" asked Dalton anxiously.

"He's only eight, and I promised him in a moment of weakness. You know kids, they never let you forget. . . ."

"Don't I know," said the man rolling his eyes.

"You've got some of your own, I believe?" Dalton asked, with interest.

"Sure. Two boys," replied Resinelli proudly.

"Really. How old are they?"

"One's fourteen and the other's twelve."

Dalton nodded. "Real handful at that age, I expect."

Obviously the mention of a big tip had helped to make the man more agreeable, although he seemed pleasant enough by nature. Dalton exchanged a few more comments before they shook hands and Resinelli went back out the door behind the counter.

Dalton turned to the fair-haired man, paid him, and obtained a receipt.

He left the building, walked back toward the parking lot, and then crossed to the other side of the street. There he waited.

At ten minutes past five he saw Resinelli's distinct figure emerge. This was the awkward part. If the man didn't have a car, Dalton would have to abandon his. He was relieved when Resinelli unlocked a red Datsun parked in front of the building. He didn't want the added complication of trailing the fellow on foot or on public transport.

He was back in his own car when the Datsun passed by. It did a U-turn and then sped away. Dalton followed quickly. As he drove, he tried to keep a maximum of two cars between himself and the target car. Traffic was heavy, and he didn't want to lose Resinelli at a red light.

He followed the Datsun, which was now headed toward the Williamsburg Bridge, crossed over, then continued on into Brooklyn. Thirty minutes later it turned into the driveway of a neat, semidetached house. Dalton pulled into the curb fifty yards back and watched as Resinelli opened the door. The house was fronted by a small, well-tended lawn, and the street had a row of similar houses on each side. Dalton waited a minute and then quickly drove past, noting the number as he went by: one forty-two. The street sign farther up said WOODLAWN PARK. He drove around the adjacent blocks, checking the street signs until he found what he wanted. He then returned to Woodlawn Park, pulled in well up from Resinelli's house, and opened a newspaper. A few other parked cars along the street and moderate traffic going by prevented him from being too conspicuous.

He didn't know how long he'd have to wait. A few people came out now and then from the neighboring houses, but none were suitable.

Forty-five minutes later a young boy of about twelve came out of the third house up from the Resinelli's. He continued on up the street and turned the corner. Dalton started the car and followed. At the end of the block he gently pulled in beside the boy. Nice and easy. He didn't want to frighten him.

"Hi," he said pleasantly. "Can you tell me where Woodlawn Park is?"

The sound of the familiar name seemed to reassure the boy.

"Sure, that's where I live. It's right down there, just around the corner." He directed Dalton back down the street.

"Much obliged," said Dalton gratefully. "I must have missed it, I'm looking for number one forty-two, the Browns'. Which end would that be?" he asked easily. Luckily the kid was bright enough.

"Well, I'm one forty-eight, so that's just down the road." He thought for a moment. "But one forty-two is the Resinelli's. There's no Browns in that house."

Dalton looked puzzled. "That doesn't sound right." He took up a large package from the passenger seat.

"'Brown' it says here on the delivery note." He paused for a moment. "I know the man had two boys in the shop with him about your age. Are there two boys at that address, by any chance? I've a feeling he called one of them Tony."

"Sure, there's two boys there but neither of them is called Tony. Mike and Chris. And their second name is Resinelli."

Dalton looked doubtfully at the package again. "No, it's definitely Brown written here." He shook his head in exasperation. "Hey, wait a minute, I think I've got the address wrong. It's Woodlawn Place, not Woodlawn Park." He clucked his tongue. "Do you know where that is?"

"Sure." The kid directed him to Woodlawn Place.

"Much obliged son." He smiled his thanks and slowly drove away.

Forty minutes later he was back in midtown Manhattan. He parked the car a few blocks from the hotel and walked to a nearby restaurant. His activities throughout the day had left him with a healthy appetite. He settled for the shell steak and baked Idaho potato, washed down with half a liter of Burgundy.

Later he walked down to Penn Station and got a timetable for the next day's train service to Washington.

Returning to his hotel he wearily went to bed. As he lay there he deliberately retraced the day's events in his mind.

He was satisfied. The first part of the snare was laid. Tomorrow he would lay the second.

• FIVE •

CHARLES DOUGLAS was a brilliant politician. Prior to becoming Prime Minister his rise to power in government had been rapid and well-planned.

His appearance was impressive. Tall and handsome with a well-brushed mane of thick black hair, his bearing commanded respect. He was not a vain man and looked on his appearance as a useful political asset; that he would have been just as successful without it, he was quite certain.

He held very strong opinions on many subjects, but was able to make these acceptable without appearing to water them down. The self-seeking fickleness of many of his colleagues was totally absent from his character. He was not afraid to take a definite public stance on an issue and stick with it. That he usually proved to have taken the right stance infuriated his enemies.

The occasional mistake that he made, he admitted frankly. These were never very serious and his frankness seemed, if anything, to enhance his public appeal. Gradually his rivals realized that this was a man who wouldn't make too many mistakes, and his status soared after a short time in opposition.

In his early days he attracted a small but extremely loyal faction of supporters. Every wolf pack has its alpha, its pack leader, and Charles Douglas fulfilled that role naturally.

His views were decidedly right-wing at a time when these views were unpopular. It was only the passage of time and the turmoils that followed which gave him the chance he so earnestly sought.

After the major rethinking that followed the party's last election defeat, Douglas had made his attempt for the leadership. His support, however, had not been sufficient to win him the contest and he had to settle for the compromise post of Deputy Leader. The relationship between Douglas and the new leader of the party was one of cautious respect. In private, the Leader had been known to express grave reservations about some of Douglas' more right-wing views.

During the years the party was in opposition, the left of the country were in their ascendancy. As economic conditions worsened, the balance finally swung too far to the left. The leader of Douglas' party was an experienced and respected politician who for years had warned of the inherent weakness of a country locked in continuous class warfare. A change was needed, a strong government that would encourage and protect the wealth-makers and equitably distribute the wealth they created. Appealing over the nominal heads of the all-powerful unions and preaching that the monsters they had created were now out of control, the Leader promised the people a new golden era, but sternly warned them that sacrifices were inevitable if real progress was to be attained.

At the end of a bitter election campaign the party was elected with a huge overall majority. Charles Douglas became Chancellor of the Exchequer in the new government.

Almost immediately after the General Election victory, the bickering between Douglas and the new Prime Minister commenced. Douglas was never happy with the pace or extent of the program of reform. He made no secret of the fact that he regarded the Prime Minister as being far too conciliatory. Their bickering became more acerbic, and many seasoned political commentators felt that it was only the Prime Minister's untimely death which ultimately prevented a major split between the two politicians. When the Prime Minister died the party turned to Douglas as the obvious choice to carry out the urgent program of industrial and economic reform.

Under his leadership the program of reform was speeded up and given more muscle. The domination of the large union blocks was directly challenged. New tough industrial laws concerning strike action were legislated and enforced. This often involved fierce confrontations, but gradually the power of the government, headed by the uncompromising Douglas, began to win the battle.

At the same time immigration laws were rigidly tightened—immigration meaning particularly Black and Asian immigration. The question of immigration from Ireland was also reviewed. Although nothing like in the past, there was still a steady flow. The identity cards that would shortly be issued would be a useful first step. All the same, it was a mine field to be negotiated with extreme caution.

The laws on immigration were already tough, but politically it was a good issue for Charles Douglas' government. Unite against the common threat and much could be accomplished in other fields. ...

Under Douglas' leadership, life began to change. Public services became more efficient, strikes were less frequent, and industrial output increased. The new stability was more than welcome and, if an individual supported the status quo, life was good. There was, however, an uneasiness in the country. People were glad to see a stop to the wastes and excesses of the past but many were apprehensive about the future. Emergency laws which the government had introduced to achieve its goals were somehow never repealed. Those who protested against the growing infringement on civil liberties were portrayed as unpatriotic and considered unsuitable for government sector employment.

The bulk of the population was only marginally affected and protest wasn't very strong. Union militants still tried to inflame their membership, but most trade unionists had had enough of confrontation and just wanted a decent job with a decent wage. And they had to admit that they were getting this under Prime Minister Douglas. ...

Charles Douglas looked at the neatly typed sheet of paper in his hand and allowed himself the rare luxury of a smile. He curtly dismissed the aide and sat down in the comfortable leather armchair behind his desk. A few seconds later he pressed the intercom buzzer.

"Yes, sir," responded his secretary crisply.

"Get Mr. Norton and tell him I want him round here at nine forty-five."

"Certainly, sir."

When the Prime Minister said nine forty-five he meant exactly that. He had extreme demands on his time and refused to waste it waiting for anybody. His associates and staff had learned very early on that the Prime Minister could be withering with latecomers.

Douglas studied the sheet carefully. It gave the results of the latest National Opinion Poll and showed his party holding an eleven percent lead on the Opposition. Last month's poll had shown a nine percent lead. An upward swing for the party at this stage in the Parliament was very satisfying.

His own personal rating was still very high, way ahead of his opposite number. Down a little from the last poll, but not significantly. If he called a shock, early election there was no doubt that his party would be swept back into power again. The thought of calling an election had fleetingly crossed his mind, but he dismissed it out of hand. The present Parliament had another year to run and it would take a very large shift in public opinion to turn him out of office then. No, he would let the Parliament run its full term.

The only slightly disturbing thing on the poll was the reply to the question about the new legislation: forty-eight percent in agreement, thirty-five percent against, and seventeen percent "don't know."

Douglas shook his head in irritation. Even after the replies along party lines had been discounted, the figure against was still much too high. The amount of "don't knows" just showed how confused the people were about the real issues. On the one hand they said that they strongly supported him and his party, and logically, the policies that the party implemented. And then they said they were worried at the measures necessary to implement these policies!

Or perhaps it was the polls themselves? Usually, they were a fair indication of public opinion on issues in between elections, but they had been proved wrong too often at the real thing for him to place much faith in them. He knew some politicians who accepted the polls as oracles; foolishly, in his opinion. When the polls were against you, you tended to question their accuracy a lot quicker than when they were favorable.

He glanced again at the paper. Five thousand people. Larger than average. A supposedly reliable cross-section of opinion round the country. The opinion of an ignorant, illiterate fool had as much validity as that of a well-informed university professor. Democracy in action, alive and kicking!

At least it wasn't as bad yet as in America, where the polls had become like another system of government. Douglas shook his head in disgust. His decisions were always based on what he thought was good for the country, not primarily to enhance his own political standing. Not that he was a fool. He was a skilled propagandist, but his driving force was the pursuit of what he knew were the right policies for the country.

Of course, the polls themselves helped to shape public opinion, and therein lay their appeal. He knew that if a person believed that the majority of other people held a certain opinion on a subject it was easier to agree with the majority than to disagree. The herd instinct was very useful if channeled correctly. . . .

The propaganda office would make a big play of this latest poll and the press would give it prominent space. Most would do so enthusiastically. After all, he *had* been good for big business, and hence their organs of information were only too willing to support him.

The Opposition press would report it reluctantly and follow as usual with a vindictive personal attack on him. They still had to report his triumphs even if it stuck in their throats. News couldn't be ignored if they wanted to sell their papers. Lately, they seemed to be getting even more hysterical in their attacks on him, galled, no doubt, by his standing in the country and their own abject failure. His recent legislation had drawn a lot of their sting. Not that anyone could accuse him of not wanting a free press. On the contrary; free, but responsible—that was the balance required. As they hadn't done it voluntarily it was necessary to legislate for it. Surely any reasonable person could see that. . . .

At exactly nine forty-five Anthony Norton was ushered into the Prime Minister's company. He was a small, well-groomed man, with a confident manner and intelligent eyes. Though not a politician, he was firmly attached to the party. He was one of Douglas' old guard and as such was a respected, though little-known, figure. He had worked in Military Intelligence throughout the Second World War, and since Douglas had become Prime Minister, had taken on the responsibility for ministerial security, with particular reference to the Irish problem. As such he acted as the communicating link between the intelligence services and the Prime Minister.

"You've seen the poll I suppose?" said Douglas directly. He never wasted time on pleasantries.

"Yes, I saw a copy in the Center," replied Norton, using the accepted term for the propaganda office. "Excellent," he added.

The Prime Minister snorted. "Fine, except for those questions on the new laws. What the hell do they want? Don't they know that you can't fight terrorism and lawlessness with one hand tied behind your back?"

Norton nodded in agreement. He knew that this was why he had been called here today. The new legislation was twin-pronged. On the one hand it strengthened the tough law and order campaign against ordinary criminals; on the other it intensified the battle against political criminals.

"The Home Office has been getting a bit of flack from the Irish Embassy again," he advised the Prime Minister. "We picked up a lot of the wrong people recently. Some of them are threatening to sue for false arrest."

"They can't," said Douglas wearily. "The new laws of arrest have been back-dated. Whatever happened before is now completely legal."

"The people we arrested don't seem to accept that," replied Norton.

"They soon will," was the Prime Minister's firm response.

"Nearly all of those arrested have had to be released," continued Norton, his voice carefully neutral.

"How on earth do they expect us to just pick up the right people?" exploded the Prime Minister angrily. "How many Irish-born people are there in this country?"

"Eight, nine hundred thousand."

"And how many more of Irish descent?"

Norton shrugged. "Who knows. Millions, I suppose."

Douglas shook his head. "I realize only a tiny percentage of them give any support to the terrorists, but it's just a needle in a haystack trying to find them. We have to pick up some harmless ones to get the odd bad one. As far as I'm concerned, that's perfectly justifiable under the present circumstances."

"It's alienated a lot of the Irish community though," said Norton, undeterred.

"Tough," snapped Douglas.

"With the American trip coming up it mightn't do any harm to make a few conciliatory noises."

Douglas looked at him for a few seconds and then nodded. "Get the Center working on it immediately."

Norton sighed inwardly. The Prime Minister was absolutely implacable about Ireland. Some years earlier, when Douglas was in opposition, Norton had once heard a Cabinet Minister suggest that they should at least consider the feasibility of a withdrawal from the damn place. Douglas had come back angrily at the man. "Never," he had said, "as long as I can influence it, will we give in to terrorism. Do you want another Cuba on our hands?"

His reference to Cuba revealed the Prime Minister's deepest fears about Ireland. The possibility of a soft underbelly on the Atlantic approaches to Britain appalled him. For years he had warned of the growing Soviet threat to world peace. The myopia of some of his colleagues over the nature of the Irish problem was utterly incomprehensible. . . .

"Have all the details been finalized for the American trip?" asked the Prime Minister.

"Just about," replied Norton. "The Yanks weren't crazy about some of our ideas, but naturally they're cooperating. Security is their main worry." A note of admiration crept into his voice.

"I must say, Prime Minister, your choice of speaking venues was quite inspired."

American public opinion was becoming increasingly anti-Douglas. The present administration had openly expressed its concern about many aspects of his legislation. In the media, words like fascist and dictator were being frequently bandied about: The British Press Agency there counteracted by constantly drawing attention to the good things that had happened in Britain—the increase in jobs and standards of living and the lack of strife which had so plagued the country in the recent past.

Douglas felt that a short visit to America with some carefully selected speaking engagements and wide-spread coverage would be well worthwhile. He had announced the possibility of a trip some months earlier.

The visit was also designed to dissuade Irish-American politicians from making unhelpful and inflammatory statements about Ireland. His predecessor's attempt at a settlement had been well received by them, but the subsequent impasse had given a new stridency to their interest.

Latest intelligence reports indicated a recent upsurge in arms-smuggling from the U.S. to Ireland. This had been reduced to a trickle in the past because of a marked drop in financial contributions from Irish-Americans. However, the premiership of Charles Douglas and subsequent disturbing reports from Ireland had undoubtably influenced this factor.

No reference was made to Ireland in the announcement of the Prime Minister's visit. A goodwill tour to present "The New Britain" was the theme.

"There's just one other thing, Prime Minister," said Norton. He coughed nervously. "We've had a tip that they may try to get you in America."

"It's logical," was the unworried reply. "They know how difficult it is here, so it would have occurred to them to try elsewhere."

Norton nodded. "We have a man out there—Maitland-Jones. He's been helping to organize security for the visit. He's had a lot of experience in the Northern Ireland security station."

A frown crossed the Prime Minister's face. "Isn't he the fellow who's been investigating the Embassy thing? Any progress on that matter?"

Norton shook his head. "Nothing definite yet."

For some months past there had been a troublesome situation in America concerning the apparent foreknowledge of certain Irish groups of proposed British press statements. Several of these had been pre-empted by well-informed Irish statements. Nothing very serious, but in the war of words, first cut was important. It pointed to a breach of security somewhere on the British side.

"This assassination tip you mentioned," said the Prime Minister, "where was it from?"

"Dublin. Since the announcement of your visit, our intelligence units have been pushing hard. One of them picked up that something was being arranged for you. They're pushing for more information, but don't want to scare off the source of the leak. They can't quite pin it down, but they think it's from a high level."

The Prime Minister snorted. "I doubt if they have the personnel or the capacity for a really serious attempt out there, but keep your men on it. If anything is going on we'll soon know about it. Somebody always talks. . . . " He glanced at his watch. "Well, keep me informed of any developments."

Norton knew that he had been dismissed.

• SIX •

KEVIN DALTON LEFT New York on the eleven-thirty A.M. Amtrak Metroliner to Washington. Earlier that morning he had returned the car to the rental agency. Just before he boarded the train at Penn Station, he removed two of the three carry-alls that he had stored in the lockers the previous day. On the ride down he never left his seat, the carry-alls and a bulky travel bag tucked securely overhead.

When the train arrived at Union Station, he disembarked and gratefully relieved himself. Once outside the station, he quickly hired a cab and directed the cabbie to a large hotel off Massachusetts Avenue.

He had selected the hotel three months earlier, on his preliminary visit. On that occasion he had spent day after day touring various sites, checking security and timetables, and noting any details that might be of subsequent use to him. For hours he had pored over the literature which was readily available to any visitor. No tourist guide ever had a more attentive listener. At the end of that period he could have easily qualified as a competent guide to the city.

When he had finally made his decision he spent another three days checking again. . . .

Dalton booked into his hotel, paid cash in advance, and quickly left.

He rented a car, using his "Alan Green" license, and locked the carry-alls in the trunk. Next he visited a number of shops and bought some specific items of clothing. The shop assistants were apparently quite used to his requests, as none of them seemed the least bit surprised.

In a luggage store he bought a good suitcase and a quantity of strong leather straps, then some sheets of pliable polyethylene in a hardware store. He visited two more stores before finally returning to his car and driving southward out of Washington.

Forty-five minutes later he turned off Interstate 95 about six miles north of the town of Fredericksburg. After three more turns he was driving along a narrow side road, with dense foliage on either side. He continued for almost a mile before eventually turning onto a small dirt track and pulling in.

As he opened the car door he heard the gunshots. He smiled as he thought of them blazing away at their mock targets. The gun club had a very large membership. It had not been difficult to determine that a competition was planned for that evening, including a clay-pigeon shoot.

He left the car and walked in a rough semicircle until he was parallel with the range. It lay to his left, completely screened by the trees and foliage. Walking behind some bushes he opened the carry-alls and removed the two Armalites. They were covered in their protective sacking which he quickly unrolled. Both guns were brand new and had been stripped down and oiled recently. He stripped them again, examined the parts, and swiftly reassembled them. The Armalite AR-150 was his favorite weapon. Small and light, but able to fire high velocity bullets, its size and effectiveness made it ideal for guerilla warfare.

He laid the guns on their sacking, and emerged from the bushes carrying two round target boards, each a foot in diameter. They were mounted on aluminium feet, with thick serrated spikes that could be pushed into the ground. He positioned the target boards alongside each other at his chosen distance and returned to the bushes.

Taking one of the Armalites, he stretched out on the ground in a supine firing position. Through a gap in the bushes he sighted on a target and fired. Over the next few minutes he fired several more shots, checking the results with binoculars. His occasional shot merged in with the bursts of gunfire from the adjacent range.

He repeated the exercise with the second Armalite, and when he was satisfied with the performance of both weapons, he retrieved the target boards. Returning behind the bushes, he stripped the guns yet again, oiled them, and replaced them in their sacking. One of them he inserted into a carry-all, which he carefully set aside.

Next he removed all the contents of the second carry-all and laid them out on a polyethylene sheet. The plastic explosive and detonators he handled with the utmost caution. Included also were two handguns with shoulder holsters. He checked that these were both fully loaded before strapping one of them on under his jacket. The explosives and detonators he then wrapped in polyethylene and replaced in the carry-all, along with the remaining handgun and the other Armalite. Finally, he unscrewed the wooden target boards from their aluminium frames and laid them on the ground.

He emerged from the bushes carrying this second carry-all, and looked around. Selecting a leafy tree, he laboriously started to climb up, taking the carry-all with him. When he was high enough up, he wedged it between two branches, using the leather straps he had bought in Washington to secure it to both branches. He pushed and tugged for a few seconds but it remained secure.

Back on the ground, he walked behind the bushes and retrieved the suitcase. Once again he hauled himself up the tree and repeated the strapping procedure with the suitcase. When he finally climbed down again, he carefully marked the bark of the tree with a large penknife and looked around for bearings. When he was satisfied that he could relocate it with ease, he returned to the bushes and collected the target boards and remaining carry-all.

Ten minutes later he was on the road back to Washington. All the activity had absorbed his attention and as he entered Washington he became aware of his hunger. He pulled in beside a large fast-food stand and ordered a steak sandwich and french fries. He ate them quickly, leaning against the counter. When he was finished, he drove back to his hotel. Before going inside, he was careful to remove the carry-all with the Armalite from the trunk. Washington's car-theft statistics soon discouraged carelessness.

He relaxed for a few hours in his room, passing the time looking at the black-and-white TV. His interest was caught by a graphic documentary on the lives of long-term prisoners in a New Jersey penitentiary. The possibility of spending a lifetime in prison was something he had faced up to a long time ago. His decision was characteristically simple; he would rather die than accept such a pathetic existence.

By the end of the documentary his relaxed mood had vanished.

In a way, he welcomed the return of the tension. It gave a valuable cutting edge to a man's behavior if channeled correctly. He looked at his watch. Ten-thirty P.M. He was conscious of hunger again. Might as well enjoy a good meal: He wouldn't be having too many for a long time to come.

The carry-all presented him with a slight problem. It was too risky to carry around with him, but he didn't want to leave it in the hotel room. He solved the problem by leaving the hotel, hiring a cab, and returning to the railway station. Here he deposited the carry-all in a locker.

Twenty minutes later he was watching the departing back of a Japanese waitress in her flowered kimono. She returned almost immediately with a carafe of white wine and a small tumbler of saki. He mixed them himself, savouring the potent combination while waiting for the food. For his main dish he had chosen raw fish on a bed of seasoned rice.

When he had finished, he paid the bill and stopped outside. It was a beautiful night, not too warm, with a slight breeze that he found invigorating. He decided against a cab and set off on the short walk to his hotel. As he walked along, he puffed on the remnants of his after-dinner cigar.

He had just turned a corner two blocks away from his hotel when the interruption came.

"Hold it, mister."

Dalton froze, completely alert now.

"Over here," the voice commanded.

Dalton looked over to his right and saw a figure standing at the entrance to a small service alley. The gun was clearly visible.

"Com'on, move it," the figure ordered.

Dalton edged into the alleyway.

Now he could see the man's face. Tall and thin with dilated pupils. The hand holding the gun was shaking. Why did he feel surprised that the guy was white?

"Okay, mister, let's see what you got. Empty your pockets out on the ground."

Speech slurred. Sounded a bit desperate.

Dalton cowered convincingly. "Please, fella, don't hurt me. I've got a wife and three kids. Take my money, but please don't hurt me." He took about eighty dollars from his trouser pockets and laid it on the ground.

"Gimme your wallet too, pal."

Dalton revised his opinion. The guy wasn't that desperate. He was trying to get everything.

"Move it," the man hissed as he cocked the gun.

Dalton weighed it up quickly. In his wallet were some documents that were vital. He just couldn't do without them. The chances were that the junkie would just take the money and dump the wallet. If the authorities got it they would try to trace the owner. When they couldn't find one it would be tricky—his photograph was on most of the documents!

"Sure, sure, take it all," he said eagerly.

Using his left hand, he removed the wallet from the inside pocket of his jacket. He handed it over to the man with a badly shaking hand. At the same time he slid his right hand inside the left breast of his jacket and closed it over the handle of his own gun.

The junkie automatically reached out to take the wallet. As he did so, Dalton jerked out the .44 from its shoulder holster and fired twice.

The explosion of the Magnum in the confined space was deafening. Both bullets entered the man's left eye and smashed him into the wall behind. As he collapsed, he overturned two garbage cans and sent them spilling along the alleyway.

Dalton moved quickly. He stooped down and retrieved the wallet and money from the body. As an afterthought, he stuffed a few dollar bills into the man's hand and closed the dead fingers over them. The police mightn't push too hard on an apparent mugging that had gone wrong.

He walked out of the serviceway, glanced around, and hurried away up the street. As he walked, he pulled a tissue from his pocket and wiped his face as well as possible. Luckily only splatters of blood. He glanced at his clothes—a red splotch here and there, but most of the skull cavity contents had gone backward.

A few minutes later he turned into his hotel, walked quickly past the night clerk, and hurried up to his room.

He immediately removed all his clothes and stuffed them into a large shopping bag. A newspaper over the top hid the contents.

He showered thoroughly and ten minutes later was stretched out on the bed. Then, switching out the light, he started to think.

Close. Too bloody close. Still it had worked out reasonably enough.

As he lay on the bed he again reviewed the day's events, seeking a flaw. When he couldn't find one he turned on his side and closed his eyes.

The snare was laid.

• SEVEN •

THE VIP LOUNGE was crammed. The battery of photographers and blinding TV lights centered on the tall handsome man seated at the interview desk. The press conference had been going on for about five minutes when the subject turned to Ireland.

"Mr. Prime Minister, your handling of the Irish problem has come in for a lot of criticism. How do you react to this?" asked one reporter.

Charles Douglas' voice was firm. "My reaction, gentlemen, is to reject such criticism as ill-informed and dangerous. As you are well aware, we are dealing with an extremely complex problem. We cannot allow our policies to be dictated by short-sighted expediency. To do so would be to abdicate all responsibility. Uninformed criticism of Her Majesty's government is just making our task that much more difficult."

"Are your anti-terrorist measures having the success you had envisaged?" asked another reporter.

"Yes, they are," replied Douglas. "We have made enormous progress, but there is still a long way to go. Let me be very clear on this point. It is vitally important that all Americans, and particularly Americans of Irish descent, understand that every cent that is contributed to terrorist organizations is directly prolonging the violence."

The room was silent as the Prime Minister pointed his finger at the assembled reporters.

"You, gentlemen of the press, have an undeniable and clear-cut duty. A duty to present these people as the heartless fiends they are. What you write is crucial to peace, so show them for what they are and not for what they claim to be."

"Turning to press relations in general, Mr. Prime Minister, it has been claimed that censorship has become an increasingly salient feature of your premiership."

Douglas spoke evenly. "Censorship is an emotive word. Certain guidelines are advised to encourage responsible media coverage. Most of these guidelines are, of course, voluntary."

"What future steps do you see as necessary to continue Britain's remarkable economic recovery?" cut in another reporter, abruptly changing the subject.

Douglas seized on the question.

"Undoubtedly we have revitalized our economy, but this is only the beginning. I am confident that my party will be in power for many years to come. We have taken the British people out of the morass of economic and spiritual decline and given them back their pride."

Fifteen minutes later the press conference ended.

On the way in from the airport the Prime Minister was in a good mood. A reasonable start, he mused. Norton had counseled against a long press conference straightaway. "Give them time to get used to you," he had advised.

Douglas had disagreed. "That's not the American way. Better to kick off sharply and keep it rolling." He had switched away from Ireland fairly quickly and was able to concentrate on the good things that had happened to Britain. That reporter had raised his question on the economy at an opportune time. Norton had told him they'd have some sympathetic reporters in if it got sticky. All in all it had gone well. . . .

The night before, in a different terminal from the one where the press conference had taken place, a young man arrived on an Aer Lingus flight from Dublin.

It was Jim Duffy's first experience with America, and he didn't like it.

He had been briefed on the job at home. Though not a stupid man, he knew his own limitations. What they were asking him to do was way out of his experience. He would gladly have given up his own life to achieve what they wanted. His worry was not for his own safety but induced by his fear of failure. They had made it clear how much was at stake, and he couldn't let them down.

His thoughts turned again to Douglas as they had so often in the last few days. Immediately he felt the rage rising in him, chasing away the doubts. God, he would do it. Just give him the chance and he'd do it. They hadn't given him any information. Just told him that he would be guided into position and guided out again afterward. He didn't waste their time with idle questions. He was used to somebody else planning a job. His role was to do it properly when the time came and let them worry about the details. They'd always looked after him before.

For the past two years he had been active in and around Crossmaglen. Crossmaglen, a small town in County Armagh, just inside the border, was his hometown. For the army it was considered the most dangerous place for a tour of duty, since the town and the hilly countryside all around it were notorious for sudden ambushes.

In the beginning, Jim Duffy treated the whole thing as a game. But on the cold October night when they collected his brother's body from the army morgue, it became deadly serious. The boy had been checking on an arms cache in a field. He was not himself a gunman. Not yet. Unfortunately for him, an army patrol had accidentially stumbled across the cache while he was there. The boy saw the patrol and tried to run. When the patrol leader challenged him and young Duffy failed to respond, the soldiers opened fire. For them it was a fair hit, a figure bending over an arms cache and then running away.

Duffy raged. He wanted to attack the barracks on his own and had to be physically restrained by three strong men. He was calmed down with the assurance that revenge would come quickly.

The face of his young brother haunted him and was only exorcised by action against the hated enemy. Within two years he had avenged his brother's death threefold, but had also lost two cousins.

In different circumstances, he might have been a contented, harmless young farmer. Now, at twenty-three, he was a dedicated fanatic and a hardened killer.

Duffy gave the taxi driver the name of a midtown motel. He looked around uncomfortably on the ride in. He was a small-town boy and found even the size of Belfast intimidating. As he moved deeper into the city, his uneasiness grew. He was glad to reach his hotel and the safety of his prebooked, prepaid room. He didn't venture out again that night. His instructions were clear.

On the same morning of the Prime Minister's press conference, Kevin Dalton had been up early. He had checked out of his hotel, driven along to a municipal dump, and thrown the bag containing the blood-splattered clothes into the rest of the rubbish. Even if it were found, it wouldn't make any difference. All of the clothes had American tags. In another section of the dump he threw away the target boards that he had used the previous day.

He returned the car to the rental agency and shortly afterward boarded the next train back to New York.

Immediately on arrival at Penn Station he went straight to the luggage area at the left. From the locker he removed the third undisturbed carry-all, the one he had not taken to Washington. This also contained an Armalite rifle. He inserted the Washington carry-all with the recently tested Armalite into the vacated locker. The switch complete, he hurried from Penn Station with the new carry-all and caught a cab to Grand Central Station. Here he quickly obtained a locker and inserted the bag into it.

As he walked out of the station he pretended to limp. It was only with apparent difficulty that he hauled himself into one of the stationary cabs. As they headed across town to the Howard Johnson Motel on Eighth Avenue, he sealed the key of the Grand Central locker into an envelope. When they arrived, he asked the cabbie to deliver the envelope to the reception desk, having already elicited the man's sympathy for his badly sprained ankle.

After a short interval, the cabbie was back and the journey continued. Four blocks further on, Dalton paid him off. He hurried back toward the motel and, from a pay phone across the street, rang the reception desk.

"Mr. Duffy, room 252 please," he requested briskly.

Duffy came on the line.

"Listen carefully," Dalton's American voice told him. "Go down to the reception desk, there's an envelope there with your name on it. It has a key in it. Once you have it, get a taxi immediately to

Grand Central Station. Go to the locker with the number on the key, remove the contents, and then return to your motel room for further instructions. Got that?"

"Yes," said Duffy, glad at last to be doing something positive. He had hardly slept that night.

"Repeat it," said the American voice.

Duffy complied.

Dalton hung up.

He quickly walked up one block and took a suitable vantage point. A minute later, he saw Duffy leave the motel and hail a cab. The cab moved away and Dalton waited patiently.

Twenty-five minutes later Duffy was back, with the carry-all firmly in his grasp.

Dalton returned to the pay phone. He dialed the number in the Bronx that he had called on his first night in New York.

"Dominic Lynch speaking," said the same distinctive voice as before.

"Send the message," Dalton said. "Send the message."

He waited beside the phone for ten minutes and then dialed the same number.

"Lynch here."

"Did you get through?" asked Dalton.

"Message delivered," said Lynch, and he waited for the abrupt click. He wasn't disappointed.

Satisfied that the transatlantic call had been delivered, Dalton walked over to a busy coffee shop across the street and slightly up from the motel. He took a window seat which allowed him a clear view of the motel entrance, ordered a coffee, and waited. . . .

In Dublin a man dialed a number in Belfast. He spoke earnestly for a few minutes and then hung up. He didn't notice the flicker of cigar ash that fell onto his trousers.

From Belfast the news went across to a large multi-storied building just south of Westminister Bridge. The SIS operative immediately lifted a red telephone and spoke hurriedly. An urgent message flashed across the three thousand miles of the Atlantic Ocean.

• • •

Dalton was on his third cup of coffee when the police cars arrived. Four of them pulled up outside the motel. No sirens. If Jim Duffy could have seen them he might have been able to do something, but his carefully chosen room had no view of the street.

Dalton sipped his coffee as he turned the pages of the *New York Post*. He didn't think it would take very long.

Six minutes later, there was a flurry of activity at the front door. Jim Duffy emerged, flanked by two burly officers and with his wrists handcuffed behind his back. They guided him to the nearest police car and bundled him unceremoniously into the back seat. The car took off with Duffy still sandwiched between the two officers.

A minute later, a plainclothes detective came out of the motel, gingerly gripping the carry-all with a white handkerchief.

Dalton paid his bill, left the coffee shop, and walked up Eighth Avenue without a backward glance. When he arrived at his own hotel he quickly collected the Nikon camera and telephoto lens that he had purchased two days earlier.

• EIGHT •

ANGELO RESINELLI LOOKED at the clock in the waiting lounge and shrugged.

The bearded guy, Green, was five minutes overdue. Not that he cared. As long as the tab was paid in advance, it was no sweat to him. Still he worked on a schedule and didn't like being kept waiting around.

A few minutes later a cab pulled up outside the pre-fab building and Dalton hurried inside, the camera swinging loosely from around his neck.

"Sorry Angelo—traffic." He smiled apologetically as he let Resinelli steer him through the glass door out into the paved area.

"I left my boy at home after all," he mouthed into Resinelli's ear above the deafening noise. "Made himself sick with nerves. I'll bring him again when he's older."

"Sure is a disappointment for him," shouted Resinelli, secretly pleased. The prospect of a young, nervous child hadn't been particularly welcome.

They reached the helicopter, and Resinelli got into the pilot's seat. Dalton sat in the back compartment and stored his camera and telephoto lens on the seat. A small, removable section separated the rear passenger area from the pilot and front passenger seats. This partition had now been removed at Dalton's request. He wanted to be able to move at will into the front of the helicopter, to the small passenger seat next to the pilot.

Dalton watched as Resinelli expertly lifted the helicopter off the landing pad. The Heliport Terminal was located on FDR Drive, just beside the East River.

Some weeks prior to his arrival in America, Dalton had chartered a small helicopter in Ireland. On that occasion he had told the charter pilot that his business required that he make a few helicopter trips. Very hush hush—the Dutch firm he was representing hadn't decided yet about the factory site. He had mentioned the fact that he had a pilot's license and expressed great interest in the technique of flying a helicopter as opposed to a plane. He had tipped the man generously after the first trip and after three trips the pilot had allowed him to sit in the control seat and instructed him in the controls.

Dalton was confident that he could fly the helicopter if he had to. He hoped it wouldn't come to that.

The helicopter rose gracefully over the East River.

"Okay, Mr. Green, you're the boss. Where do we go first?" asked Resinelli cheerfully.

"Fly to the United Nations," said Dalton.

The helicopter headed up river.

"The other day you mentioned a prize being offered by a magazine, Photo something . . . ?" asked Resinelli conversationally.

"*Photography Today,*" replied Dalton enthusiastically. "It's one of the most popular photography magazines in the country."

"How much did you say the prize was?" asked Resinelli as if he didn't really believe what Dalton had told him on their last meeting.

"The first prize is three thousand dollars."

"Jeez," the pilot whistled, "just for some pictures! Makes you wonder. . . ."

"Not for 'some pictures,'" returned Dalton, slightly miffed. "For the most unusual and aesthetic photography of contemporary architecture," he intoned, as if quoting from an entry form. "Photography is my only hobby. I spend most of my spare time at it. I've won quite a few amateur competitions before," he finished proudly.

"Lot of expense to go to all the same," said Resinelli disinterestedly.

"Well, besides the unusual aerial angles I hope to capture the sunlight falling the right way and creating some atypical shadow formations," enthused Dalton happily. "You will be able to hold the helicopter very steady, I hope." He let a note of anxiety creep into his voice.

"You could put a pitcher of water on the floor and not a drop would spill," said Resinelli, with the sure tone of a man in total command of his profession.

They flew around the United Nations for a few minutes, Dalton snapping away rapturously through the open side window of the helicopter.

"That's beautiful. Can you just hold it here?" he shouted above the propeller noise. "Okay, that's great," he said shortly. He checked his watch. "Let's head back down river now," he said, moving easily into the passenger seat.

They moved quickly along the side of the river and eventually reached the Wall Street area. Dalton got Resinelli to hold the helicopter steady at a number of buildings as he clicked busily away.

"Let's move along to the World Trade Center," he said, moving back into the rear seat and inserting a fresh load of film into the camera.

At the World Trade Center, the pilot repeated the procedure of hovering steadily while Dalton took his photographs. Again he checked his watch.

"Okay, that's fine."

The helicopter moved toward the tip of Battery Park.

"How long before we head back to the landing pad?" prodded Dalton.

"We've got five more minutes, then we gotta go," replied Resinelli.

"Where will we go next?" mused Dalton, pretending to be temporarily at a loss.

The Statue of Liberty dominated the view.

"You wanna go 'round the Lady?" responded Resinelli, nodding toward the statue just into the harbor.

"Well, I don't really think it would qualify as contemporary architecture," said Dalton doubtfully. He looked at his watch. "Still might as well fly over and have a look." He was glad Resinelli had bitten. If possible, he didn't want to suggest it himself.

As they moved out into the harbor he quickly fitted the telephoto lens to the camera.

"Just fly around it once and we'll go home," he ordered. "I'm eager to get these other ones developed."

They flew around the statue counterclockwise. As they rounded toward the front, Dalton's eyes picked out the workmen erecting the temporary wooden platform at the base. Quickly raising his camera, he zoomed in on the platform and snapped it once.

The helicopter moved away and headed back up toward the East River.

"Well, are you satisfied with your photographs?" asked Resinelli in a slightly patronizing voice.

"Marvelous angles," enthused Dalton. "I really hope I got those shadows on the UN building." His voice was full of admiration. "Angelo, you really know how to fly this thing."

Resinelli accepted the flattery as his due.

As they headed back toward the helicopter terminal Dalton stared contemplatively at the back of the pilot's head. He hoped he wouldn't have to kill him.

There was no doubt in his mind that Resinelli could handle the flying part satisfactorily. He had considered getting an outside pilot but the difficulties precluded that—his biggest objection was the risk of a leak. Besides, he wanted one of the easily identifiable red-and-white tourist helicopters.

He was aware of a number of flaws in his plan. The biggest could be Resinelli himself.

He wanted a lever on the man. A gun nuzzling in the small of the back provided a strong enough lever for most people. Still, a young guy with no great responsibilities might just be courageous enough to try something stupid. He would have to tell the pilot what he intended to do early on in the flight, so that when the actual moment came the fellow would know exactly what was required of him. Unfortunately, this early knowledge would give the pilot time to think. Shutting the radio off would obviously sever any communication with the helicopter base. After a few minutes, the pilot would realize that if Dalton shot him, the helicopter would crash, in which case both of them would die. Unless, of course, Dalton could fly it himself. Therefore, he would advise the pilot early on that he could fly the helicopter if necessary.

The pilot would soon realize, though, that even if Dalton was telling the truth and could fly the helicopter, it was unlikely that he would be able to fly it with the precision required, and successfully complete his mission at the same time.

A brave man might reason that there would be absolutely nothing to be gained by killing him. In fact, doing that would insure the failure of the mission. It was just possible that such a man would not cooperate, even with the threat of the gun.

No, he had to have a pilot who would be so scared of the consequences of refusal that he would do exactly as he was ordered.

He had prebooked the pilot and helicopter for the following morning, as well as for today. Tomorrow, when he boarded the helicopter, he would threaten the pilot at gunpoint immediately after takeoff. He would tell him that his house in Woodlawn Park had been watched for the last two months, and would call the pilot's children by name and tell him that his two sons were at that moment being held by his accomplices. If Resinelli did exactly as he was told they would be released later that morning, completely unharmed.

If he did not cooperate, his wife would soon be burying three coffins. The pilot would need to use all his skill with the helicopter to insure his children's release and his own safety.

Dalton estimated that Resinelli would not take the chance that he was bluffing. The pilot would do as he was told.

At the Statue of Liberty tomorrow morning the Prime Minister would make a short speech. Security would be foolproof on the ground, but they would still be vulnerable from the air. . . .

The other flaw in his plan was the likely presence of police helicopters circulating over the target area. Knowing that they had arrested a potential assassin the day before might put them a little off-guard. A commonplace tourist helicopter doing its usual tour could get in without too violent a challenge.

He would order Resinelli to fly around the statue counterclockwise in a tight circle. Once he had made the hit he would head for a landing site he had chosen on the Lower East Side. He estimated that he could be at that site within two minutes flying time after the hit. He expected helicopter pursuit and harassment. To actually down his helicopter they would have to shoot directly at the pilot as surveillance helicopters were not fitted with cannon. If it came to it, and if a police helicopter threatened, he would try to kill the pilot. He would back himself in that sort of situation.

His landing site was on a vacant lot that he had previously examined at ground level. A subway stop which was both local and express was located twenty yards around the corner. The short time involved and the fact that they wouldn't know his landing site would make it impossible for them to direct any police cars to the site in time. Once he got into the subway system he knew how to lose them.

He estimated that he had an even chance of making the hit and getting out afterward. Very good odds, considering the target. . . .

The helicopter arrived smoothly back on the pad. Dalton collected his equipment and jumped out. He kept talking about his tremendous photographs as they walked the short distance to the departure lounge.

Once inside he thanked Resinelli and gave him a twenty-dollar tip.

"Marvelous, just marvelous. I'll see you tomorrow morning, Angelo," he said as he pressed the bills into Resinelli's hand.

Nice guy, thought Resinelli as Dalton went out the door.

• NINE •

HELEN TAVERNE FOUGHT down the waves of panic that suddenly engulfed her. Go away, oh, please go away, she pleaded silently.

The telephone refused to stop.

Pull yourself together, she told herself. It might not even be them. She glanced at the clock. Seven P.M. Luckily she was alone. Philip had had to return to the Consulate tonight. Later on he would be going to the reception for the Prime Minister.

Since last night she had been pretending to be ill. When she had told her husband that she just couldn't accompany him, he had been very concerned and ready to skip going himself. She had persuaded him that it was very important that he attend. A rising young diplomat couldn't miss such an important occasion. She told him that she would take some sleeping tablets, go to bed with a hot drink, and see the doctor in the morning if she didn't feel better. Reluctantly he had agreed to leave her. It would never have occurred to Philip Taverne that his wife was lying.

She picked up the phone.

"Mrs. Taverne?" asked the caller.

Not the usual voice.

"Yes?" she replied hesitantly.

"My name is Palmer. A mutual friend asked me to call you. He said you had something you wished to discuss with me."

Palmer! That was the code name they'd given *her*.

Hang up, she urged herself. Just hang up!

"Yes," she replied dully.

"I'm afraid I can't come over, but could you meet me in Ray's Pizza Parlor in the Village at ten o'clock tonight? It's on the corner of Eleventh Street and Sixth Avenue. Do you know it?"

The voice was pleasant enough but it was obviously an order and not a request.

"Yes, I know it," she replied, almost inaudibly.

"Fine, ten o'clock, then. I'll look forward to seeing you."

The line went dead.

Kevin Dalton walked away from the pay phone and headed back to his hotel. The woman had sounded strung-out and jumpy. Natural under the circumstances, he supposed. She'd been leaned on a lot, but not too much. They didn't want to break her, just make her very willing to cooperate. She was a potentially weak link in the chain, but a vital one. It was unlikely that she herself knew just how vital.

Helen Taverne replaced the receiver and looked at herself in the mirror. The tears had started to trickle slowly down her face. She walked away and sat down listlessly on the sofa. Suddenly her despair overwhelmed her and she burst into an uncontrollable wave of sobbing.

Helen had married when she was thirty-one. She was a rather ordinary-looking girl, but had always looked after her appearance and tried to emphasize her best features, notably her beautiful chestnut hair.

Her husband was three years older than she. Philip Taverne was an intelligent and well-educated man with a good future ahead of him. He was of a serious disposition and held very strong religious beliefs.

They had been introduced at a party in Chelsea. Helen was working for a large publishing firm at the time, and one of her colleagues had invited her to the party. She had been working for the publishing firm for over four years and thoroughly enjoyed her work. It compensated for what was a rather lonely social life as she was not very gregarious. Before joining the firm, she had tried a number of different jobs but had never been completely happy with them.

She had been born in Dublin, the third of six children. Her parents were ambitious and had scrimped and saved to send her to the university. She had felt a sense of obligation to them ever since.

Often, the burden of eternal gratitude irritated her, but she quickly stemmed this feeling as being unworthy of a good daughter.

She had never told them of the trouble. They would never understand.

When she was seventeen she had gone out on a date, her third date ever. She had been given too much to drink and later driven to a deserted beach on the North Side of Dublin. She knew that she shouldn't have gone but the drink had lowered her resistance and she felt happy and carefree. She had listened to the young man's soothing words and had been intoxicated by the combination of romantic lies and the moonlight that bathed the sweep of Dublin Bay.

When it was over she had cried and begged to be taken home. The young man, his ardor satiated, had driven her back silently.

When she missed her period, she was panic-stricken. Finally, when she knew it was not just worry that made her late, she had gone for a pregnancy test. The fifteen minutes she spent waiting for the results were the longest of her life. When the test finally came back as positive, she felt that her life had come to an end.

Her parents were strict Catholics. They would never accept that such a thing could happen to their daughter.

She contacted the young man and told him. He hung up. Only when she threatened to come around to his house and confront his parents did he agree to meet her.

When they met at a small Grafton Street café he immediately insisted on an abortion. The very thought horrified her. Her upbringing and religion had taught her that what he suggested was murder. She fled the café in horror.

For a month she did nothing but keep her secret to herself, and she lost sixteen pounds with worry. The weight loss was passed off to her parents by inventing a ficticious diet.

Two weeks later she telephoned the young man and met him again. He told her that she would have to go to London for the abortion.

She explained to her parents that a friend had invited her to England for a week's holiday. She traveled alone on the mail boat from Dun Laoghaire, and, two days later, she had her abortion in a small clinic in Bromley.

Back in Ireland again, she eventually completed her Bachelor of Arts degree and shortly afterward emigrated to England permanently.

She never saw the young man again.

At the Chelsea party where he had met his wife, Philip Taverne had not been enjoying himself. He was a disciplined and strong-willed man, disliking any sort of excess in himself or others. A practicing Roman Catholic and a deeply moral man, it was only his kind and thoughtful nature that saved him from being an insufferable puritan.

He disapproved of the large amount of alcohol that was being consumed at the party. It was only reluctantly that he had agreed to come in the first place. He was introduced to Helen and was immediately attracted by her quiet and dignified manner. They had chatted about books and music and found that they shared many interests. Philip had sensed that she was as guarded as he and found this appealing. He had timidly asked for her telephone number and she had just as timidly given it.

The months passed by and the relationship slowly developed. It was not a strongly romantic attachment, but just as deep and far more lasting. They genuinely liked each other and love came later. When it did it was based on a core of mutual trust and respect.

Helen never told Philip of the abortion. She knew his strict views on the subject and was convinced that if he ever found out it would mean the end of their relationship. She didn't want to lose him.

They were married six months later in University College Church in Dublin.

It was a good marriage, with both sets of parents approving, although Helen's parents weren't too happy about Philip's diplomatic career, with its regular domestic upheavals. However, they knew that she was happy, and although they would never say it, were slightly relieved that she had found a partner.

Philip had been attached to the Consulate in New York for three years. For two and a half of those years Helen had been blissfully happy.

Then the phone call came.

• • •

She never knew how they found out, and they never told her. One day she received a phone call and was told that the caller had some important information for her. She was given a telephone number, advised not to mention it to her husband for her own sake, and ordered to ring the number from a public phone. She was about to tell the caller that she would do no such thing when he mentioned one word.

Abortion.

She rang the number.

All that would be required from her was some harmless information. Part of her husband's job in the Consulate involved the dissemination of information about Britain to the American press. He often had papers at home and talked freely about his work to his wife. Up to then, she had only half listened, but now she became very attentive.

She was told she had to ring the same number at least every two weeks, but always to use a public phone. They never contacted her at home again.

Generally, the information she gave them was not of major importance, though it did give them a useful advantage in counter-propaganda.

When she had last phoned, they had warned her to be home on that one particular night. They wanted some more information, specifically about the Prime Minister's tour. They told her that they were arranging some counter-demonstrations for him. As an extra incentive they also mentioned her elderly parents in Dublin. Helen got the message and cooperated.

She wanted to keep her world intact.

· TEN ·

WILLIAM MAITLAND-JONES was worried. Something was wrong, but he couldn't quite pin it down. The harder he tried, the more elusive it became. He deliberately pushed it out of his mind and reflected back over the last few weeks.

He knew that he had failed and it rankled. He was an experienced and realistic man, and he accepted that one could not always be successful. In his long career, however, he had been successful often enough to dislike the occasional failure. He was honest enough to admit that it was basically a question of pride. Pride and professionalism. A good professional tried for one hundred percent success all the time. If he achieved ninety-five percent success, he concentrated on the five percent failure and studied the reasons for it.

He had arrived in New York seven weeks earlier. It had looked like a fairly easy administrative assignment at the time and a welcome break from the grinding intensity of Northern Ireland. For some months past, information that had not been publicly released appeared to have filtered into the wrong hands. Nothing particularly important but in the finely drawn tactics of propaganda warfare, they could not afford to give anything away.

Maitland-Jones regarded himself basically as a security officer. He had tested and polished his techniques in Kenya and Aden. At the commencement of the troubles in Ireland he had been brought in very early on. For years he had been involved in the thrust and counterthrust of military and civilian intelligence. He did not concern himself with the political arguments, and changes of government meant little to his activities. His role was clear-cut. He became an expert in the history, organization, and, as far as possible, the personnel of the enemy. He tried to put himself in their place, to gauge their reactions to events, and hence the counterreactions of the government forces. He was very successful at his job. Many terrorists and would-be terrorists were lying in graveyards or spending long spells in prison as a result of his activities. He helped to develop and nurture effective intelligence surveillance. If dissent could be fostered among rival enemy groups, as so often it could, Maitland-Jones and his team encouraged it. They had a generous supply of funds and used them liberally.

Maitland-Jones had an inexhaustable memory for seemingly insignificant trivia and knew as much about counter-terrorism as any man alive. The trouble was that the terrorist personnel changed so quickly, either through army successes or the natural attrition of time, that it was difficult to keep on top of the situation.

When he arrived in New York he had set about his task quickly and methodically. The Ministry was anxious to clear up the annoyance as swiftly as possible in view of the Prime Minister's impending visit. Maitland-Jones' presence in the Consulate was easily attributable to the planning of security for the Prime Minister's trip, which was partly true anyway.

First, he had examined the personal files of the entire consular staff. Naturally, every one of them had had top security clearance before being accepted into such a delicate profession. He immediately eliminated those who had no access, or only partial access, to the information that had been filtered to the other side.

After two days of intensive study, he had whittled the number of people with access to all of the information down to seven. One of these was the Consul himself, a former high-ranking army officer and a minor member of the British aristocracy. Maitland-Jones logically eliminated him.

One of the others was not on the staff when the earlier leaks had occurred, so he was eliminated also, at least temporarily.

Maitland-Jones' initial investigation was therefore concentrated on a short list of five.

Three of them had joined the consular staff only nine months before, when the size of the Consulate had been increased. The leaks had commenced about three months later.

Another had been there for nearly three years. His wife was Irish-born, which was interesting, but not necessarily significant. Naturally she had had full security clearance before her husband had been posted to his present assignment and had passed through with no problems. Discreet inquiries had established that she was extremely contented with her lot and had never expressed the slightest interest in the Irish troubles. Maitland-Jones had in fact met her at an official function soon after his arrival. Quiet—mousy, even—had been his judgment.

The fifth one, and Maitland-Jones' own choice, was a thirty-eight-year-old bachelor with a taste for the finer things in life. Handmade shirts and shoes, beautifully tailored suits, and a penchant for expensive cars were usually beyond a junior diplomat's salary. A discreet inquiry in England revealed that the man had no independent income. In Maitland-Jones' considerable experience the foremost cause for betrayal of trust was greed.

Examination of the bank accounts of each of the subjects proved fruitless. None of the accounts showed any unusual lodgments or sudden dischargement of large debts, though the bachelor was well overdrawn. Maitland-Jones didn't think it would be that easy but he was constantly amazed at just how stupid some people could be. They seemed to think that by simply lodging hot money in the bank, it became undetectable.

Each of their homes, supplied rent-free by the Consulate, was entered secretly and thoroughly searched by experts. Another blank.

Maitland-Jones was not in the least bit discouraged. He knew that if a person took even the most obvious precautions, detection could be avoided for a long time.

The next stage was routine wiretapping and round-the-clock surveillance of the suspects and their homes. An order was sought and obtained for authorization of the wiretaps.

This produced a result almost immediately. Within three days he knew why the third suspect had never married. They tried to screen homosexuals early on, but were not always successful. The blackmail risk was obviously unacceptable. Maitland-Jones did nothing with the information. If the suspect was his man, he wanted to make it absolutely indisputable. One way or another, the fellow's diplomatic career was finished.

Maitland-Jones received daily written reports on the tapping and surveillance activities. He quelled his disgust on reading the main suspect's amorous telephone conversations.

Since the security officer's arrival there had been no new leak. He was fairly certain that those under surveillance could not be aware that they were being watched and therefore hadn't been scared off. He decided to flush the suspect out.

The homosexual diplomat was provided with some interesting information, apparently valuable but in fact totally false. Nobody else received the same information. Maitland-Jones waited for a week, carefully studying the daily reports.

Still nothing broke.

He began to feel the first gnawings of frustration. Optimism of an early result had now faded. He would have to try the same technique on the others and just wait and see. The fact that the Prime Minister had arrived and the person responsible for the disclosures was still undetected magnified his failure.

Maitland-Jones rubbed his tired eyes and checked his watch. Nine twenty-five P.M. Time to get ready for the reception. Always a methodical man, he tidied his desk prior to departure.

As he pushed his chair back to stand up, the reason for his earlier worry suddenly came to him. It had to do with that man Duffy whom the police had arrested that afternoon. The consular staff had been talking about it all evening. Arrested in his hotel with a loaded rifle! Didn't know what hit him till the cuffs were on!

Maitland-Jones sat down again and looked on his desk for the copy of the preliminary police report. He had ordered a copy as soon as he heard of the arrest. Although his main preoccupation recently had been to locate the consular leak, he was always very conscious of security for the Prime Minister's visit.

There was something in that report which jarred. A lifetime of intelligence work told him that it was just too easy. He started to read.

First of all, the man had been arrested as a result of a tip in Ireland. Fair enough, that wasn't what worried him. God knows he'd had enough tips himself. He read further.

Of course, it was the passport! The report had stated that Duffy had come to America on his own passport. He knew the enemy. If they wanted an assassin to come in and remain undetected, why the hell would they let him use his own passport?

He looked at another report which had been Telexed across from

London an hour ago. It contained all the known facts on Jim Duffy. Close relatives, including one brother, killed by the army. Known enemy activist. Suspected of at least two killings.

Jesus, how long did they expect him to survive in America without being discovered? All it would take was a slight indiscretion on someone's part in Ireland and they would locate him without any trouble. Which was exactly what had happened.

His own passport, for Christ's sake! It just didn't wash.

His mind was grappling with the problem when a light tap came on the door. He looked up, slightly startled.

"Come in," he invited.

A severe-looking middle-aged secretary entered and gave him an envelope sealed with red wax. He signed the form, thanked her, and absentmindedly slit it open, his mind still dwelling on the Duffy incident. The envelope contained the day's visual and audio surveillance reports on the suspects in the Consulate. He glanced through them somewhat lethargically. Suddenly he stiffened. He was looking for something unusual and now he had it.

The telephone conversation between Helen Taverne and the unknown caller. What was said seemed fairly innocuous on the face of it. However, his previous inquiries about Helen Taverne had revealed her to be a quiet, home-loving person not given to going into Greenwich Village to meet somebody at nighttime. And certainly not on the night of the most important consular reception of the year.

What was to be discussed that was so important to take her all the way to Greenwich Village to meet a man whom she had never met before?

Maitland-Jones picked up the special telephone at his left side. A minute later he was speaking to a man seated in a car discreetly parked near the Taverne apartment.

"Has Mrs. Taverne left the apartment yet?" he asked without preamble.

"Yes, sir. She left in a cab about ten minutes ago."

"Damn!" Maitland-Jones slammed down the phone, grabbed his coat, and raced outside. A passing cab made him decide against using one of the cars in the Consulate carpool. As it moved off he checked his watch. Nine fifty-five P.M. Christ, he'd never make it....

• ELEVEN •

KEVIN DALTON POSITIONED himself near Ray's Pizza Parlor and waited. He had chosen it because of its good access and because it was always crowded.

He reconsidered the question of Helen Taverne. He regretted what he would have to do, but there was no other way. His hand touched the handle of the thin-bladed switch knife in his pocket. He would sever both carotid arteries, and death would be quick and merciful. Taking her handbag would make it seem like another robbery that had turned into a murder.

He had to have the information, but he couldn't take the risk of her talking afterward.

He knew the broad outlines of the Prime Minister's tour, the cities and most of the venues, but the exact timetable would not be finalized until Douglas had actually arrived in America. Dalton had to have that timetable. The tour would be extensive and exhausting, and Douglas' time would be strictly rationed.

He knew that tomorrow's event at the Statue of Liberty was planned for the morning, as it had been arranged before the Prime Minister's arrival. But he didn't know the exact time. He had hired Resinelli and his helicopter for the entire morning. Since he would only get one chance to fly over the target area, it had to be when the Prime Minister was speaking on the wooden platform. The same-numbered helicopter flying near the site for too long would immediately arouse suspicion. The TV crews and newspaper reporters would be out there early on and would have a good idea of the Prime Minister's schedule, but Dalton had to be more exact than that. The duration of the speech would determine the amount of leeway he had. The longer it lasted, the better his chances of successfully timing the attempt.

It was a pity that he would have to kill her. Unfortunately, he had no choice. . . .

Helen Taverne paid off her cab and walked quickly to the meeting site. The thought of eating pizza made her nauseous, but she knew she couldn't just wait there empty-handed. She entered the pizza parlor, bought a slice, and walked over to the middle counter. As usual the place was full, and nobody paid her the slightest heed. She glanced around but couldn't see anyone looking at her. She felt a sudden surge of hope. Perhaps they had changed their minds and nobody would come?

A bearded man, dressed in a working-man's blue jacket, left the serving counter after having collected his pizza, and glanced around for a free space. He moved easily in at Helen's counter, just one person away from her. She glanced quickly at him, but he seemed intent on leisurely chewing his pizza. He started to read a partly folded newspaper. The person between them finished his pizza, threw the paper plate in the refuse bin, and walked out. The gap between her and the bearded man seemed to narrow as he leaned over for some seasoning.

Dalton waited for another minute. He had watched her arrival and had waited until he was reasonably sure she hadn't been followed.

He spoke softly, without looking at her.

"Don't look at me, Mrs. Taverne."

She quickly looked forward again after the involuntary sideways glance.

He spoke so low that she strained to catch the words.

"Answer my questions with one word, whenever possible," he whispered. "Don't nod your head, understand?"

She started to nod her head in agreement but just managed to stop herself. His questions came quickly and were very specific.

Not once did he even glance at her.

Maitland-Jones dropped the cab off on Eleventh Street and walked across to the pizza parlor. He looked through the large glass window at the front and immediately spotted Helen Taverne. She was at the second counter facing away from him, her beautiful chestnut hair making her easy to identify.

He looked at the people beside her but couldn't see anyone talking to her. He went inside, bought a slice, and stood at the first circular counter. He was careful to avoid looking at her. It was quite possible that she would remember him from their previous brief meeting. He strained his ears but couldn't hear anything. He could just see the side of Helen's face and saw her lips occasionally pursing. She was talking, he was certain of it. It had to be someone just beside her. Again he examined her neighbors. To her left was a young, jeans-clad teenage girl. After a glance he dismissed her. To her right was a bearded fellow reading his newspaper.

Maitland-Jones concentrated on him. He couldn't see the man's face and the beard blurred his mouth. Christ, it was no good! He was sure she was talking to the bearded man, but he'd have to get a better angle. The fellow looked roughly dressed. What would he have in common with Helen Taverne?

He walked out of the pizza parlor and turned down the corner, the half-eaten slice held absently in his hand. Through the large glass side-window of the parlor, he had a full view of the patrons eating inside. The street was crowded with people strolling leisurely by, and he was able to stand beside the window without being too conspicuous.

He looked in at Helen and the man beside her. They were about thirty feet away from him. Now he could see them full on. He noticed the man's lips moving occasionally. It looked as if the fellow were reading his newspaper and unwittingly mouthing the words to himself. He even changed the pages once. Looked authentic enough. Maitland-Jones studied the face closely. There was something vaguely familiar about it. He had seen it somewhere before, but where? In Ireland, he was sure of that. He let his mind drift back over the years.

A photograph, that was it. He'd seen a photograph of the man somewhere.

Years back one of the enemy's political offices had been raided. At the actual time of the raid, the people in the office were burning as many of their documents as they could, possibly alerted by a tip-off. Whatever remained unburned was taken away and sifted through. Photographs in particular were closely examined. It was around the time of the Bloody Sunday incident in Derry, which had provoked an influx of bitter young men into the Organization.

Maitland-Jones looked again at the bearded man. Mentally he stripped the beard off and made him a bit younger. Could it be the same fellow? He had never surfaced in his reports again, and Maitland-Jones had forgotten about it. Except for the photo. God only knows where it would be after all these years. They had not seriously started to computerize their information until shortly after that.

He thought back to Ireland again. For some years they had had occasional whiffs of information about a man working independently of the movement and carrying out his own operations. For most of the killings of their members, the security forces had a good idea of the individuals responsible. After a few weeks or months somebody always talked, and they then got a reasonable idea of the men involved. But Maitland-Jones was aware that too many of the killings couldn't be attributed to anyone in particular.

Regarding the supposed "loner," he had received a few possible names but they had never checked out. He had sent one of his best undercover men, an SAS volunteer, down across the border to try and locate this unknown man. If he even existed. Once located, the agent had explicit instructions to silence him. He never returned, and his body was never found.

Maitland-Jones remembered his earlier doubts about Jim Duffy's arrest that afternoon. It made sense now. The sloppy passport incident, the leak in Ireland—they wanted Duffy arrested! To clear the way for the real assassin?

He fought down the feeling of excitement rising in him. Christ, was it possible after all these years?

Maitland-Jones made a mistake. He had become so absorbed in his thoughts that he had stared fixedly at Dalton for almost a minute.

Dalton became aware of the middle-aged man standing outside the large side window and apparently peering in his direction. He examined him carefully through the glass.

Helen Taverne's eyes followed his glance. She started involuntarily when she saw Maitland-Jones.

Dalton spoke softly.

"Do you know him?" he whispered without looking at her.

"Yes, he's been involved with the Consulate for a few weeks."

Dalton glanced back at the man. His eyes took in the half-eaten pizza in the man's hand. So he'd been inside the pizza parlor. Had he heard anything?

At that moment Maitland-Jones looked straight into Dalton's eyes. Dalton returned the other's gaze with a level stare.

Maitland-Jones looked quickly away and stared unseeingly into the street. Damn! It looked like the fellow had spotted him. He waited another half minute, and then glanced back. The fellow was looking at his paper again. The security officer was undecided on what to do. Jesus, he wasn't even armed. For this American assignment he had dispensed with the Walther p.k. Automatic that he routinely carried in Northern Ireland. If the fellow had noticed him it would be foolish to try and challenge him alone. He needed back-up. He looked up and down the street for a pay phone but couldn't see one. He would have to chance leaving the man unobserved while he phoned for help.

Maitland-Jones moved away from the pizza counter.

Dalton was looking at the paper while keeping his lateral vision totally concentrated on the man outside. Quickly he weighed up the options. The watcher had obviously known that Helen was coming to the pizza parlor. He hadn't followed her, he was reasonably sure of that. Therefore, either she'd told him where she was going, or they must have tapped her phone. He didn't think she'd told them.

The man had to be in security. His trained descriptions could be as good as a photograph. Also, he could confirm that Helen had in fact met him and she was bound to be questioned.

"Listen carefully," Dalton said to her. "If they ask you, deny that you ever met anyone here tonight. Say that nobody turned up. They won't believe you, but they can't prove otherwise. Do you understand? Make up some excuse for being here." He thought furiously. He knew she worked as a part-time reader for a New York publishing firm. "Say you were arranging to have a look at some important documents. Give the impression that you thought they could be pretty valuable, but of doubtful legal origin, and hence the roundabout way of meeting. Stick to that no matter what they say and you'll be okay. I'll take care of your friend."

Helen nodded, her eyes wide with fear.

It was weak, but better than nothing. He had to buy time. He saw the man move away from the window and started out of the pizza parlor after him.

Maitland-Jones moved along crowded Sixth Avenue, searching for a phone. He gave a quick backward glance over his shoulder. The fellow was coming after him! His search for a phone intensified, but the only one that he passed was in use. He looked around again. The fellow was gaining.

He turned at the next corner, onto a residential street, and started to run. Although not a young man, he exercised with a daily game of squash and was quite fit for his age. He ran almost a hundred yards before looking back. The bearded fellow was also running!

As he ran, the number of people in the streets thinned out. He realized that he had made a mistake. Turning aimlessly like that without really thinking where he was going. Stupid! He was no longer looking for a phone. The important thing now was to get back and warn them.

His heart was pounding in his ears, but he forced himself to think. He must direct his run. If his suspicions were correct and if he didn't lose his pursuer, he was a dead man. He had to get back to tell them. . . .

Dalton was gaining.

As he pursued Maitland-Jones he pulled a white handkerchief from his pocket and held it in one hand. Seventy yards.

The man was moving well for his age. Dalton increased his speed. Sixty yards.

The man glanced frantically behind him. Dalton could see the flush of exertion and fear on his face. Fifty yards.

Maitland-Jones made a sharp right turn at the next corner onto Seventh Avenue. Dalton raced after him. As he turned the corner he saw his quarry heading toward the steps of the subway entrance on Fourteenth Street.

Maitland-Jones charged down the steps and leap-frogged over the turnstiles. As he landed he stumbled dangerously, but just managed to right himself. The life-giving adrenaline surged through him, pushing him on. He prayed silently. Oh, God, please let me see a transit cop!

Dalton leap-frogged after him.

Maitland-Jones ran down another flight of steps, passed through a large opening, and onto a platform. A train stood there with one remaining door open, beckoning him to safety! There might be a cop on it. Someone had told him that because of the subway violence, nearly all the trains had cops on them these days.

The last passengers had already boarded the train. As he charged toward the open door, his mouth tried to form words, but his lungs were unable to provide the air. The door started to close when he was five yards away. He made one final, desperate lunge and his momentum carried him through the opening and into the trian.

The door shut firmly behind him.

He lay on the floor, drained and gasping for air. The other passengers stared open-eyed at him. Thanks be to Jesus! He was safe!

Dalton, following some yards behind, had come through the platform opening just in time to see his quarry's frantic dive into the train. As he ran toward the door he pulled out his gun, using the handkerchief to grip the butt. He reached it as the train started to move gently forward. Through the glass of the door, he could see Maitland-Jones lying spread-eagled on the floor. Quickly, he sighted and fired. The bullet shattered the glass but was deflected from its target.

The train slowly began to gather speed as Dalton jogged alongside. It had fifteen yards to go before the car carrying Maitland-Jones disappeared into the safety of the tunnel. Through the fist-sized hole that the bullet had made, he fired two more shots at the helpless figure on the floor.

As the car disappeared into the darkness he heard the screams of horror drifting back through the tunnel.

More passengers had come through the opening and onto the platform. Dalton turned and sprinted back toward the exit, keeping his head well tucked down. Nobody tried to stop him as he ran. He was well up the stairs before he heard the cries coming up after him.

"Shooting."

"Someone get a cop." A woman's hysterical voice.

As he reached the top of the stairs he turned the corner toward the platform exit gate. Suddenly the breath was knocked completely out of his body. He had collided with an enormously fat woman who was carrying three paper bags! Both of them lay helplessly winded on the ground. One of her bags contained some large red apples, which began to roll across the station floor.

The suddenness of the collision had sent the gun flying from his hand and bouncing back down the steps.

He disentangled himself from the woman and picked himself shakily up.

A transit cop who had appeared through one of the other passageways came running over, his attention drawn by the shouts and then the collision. As he approached, Dalton gestured frantically toward the stairs.

"Shooting. There's been a shooting down there. Hurry!"

The cop looked automatically toward the stairs, and as he turned his head Dalton kicked him viciously in the knee. The cop collapsed in agony. Dalton turned, burst through the exit gate, and raced up the steps out of the station. He ran nonstop for four hundred yards. Finally he stopped and listened.

No sounds of pursuit. He decided against a cab as he walked quickly away. Shortly afterward, he was sitting on a bus heading uptown. At Times Square he left the bus and walked the rest of the way to his hotel.

Back at the hotel he switched on the television and caught a news bulletin. Nothing. He switched channels regularly for the next three-quarters of an hour. Finally he was rewarded.

The statement was brief and factual.

"A middle-aged man was shot and killed on a subway train in Greenwich Village tonight. The police have identified him but do not wish to release his name until the next of kin have been informed. They have a number of eyewitnesses to the slaying and are confident of an early arrest. The victim was apparently pursued by his killer into the station and shot on board the train." The report concluded with a brief, patchy description of the killer.

Nothing else. Should he remain in the hotel tonight? He thought briefly of leaving, but decided to stay put. It was unlikely that they would have anything to work on yet except the gun. Of course, it was only a matter of time. It would be better to risk the hotel for the night rather than go elsewhere.

It was a large hotel with many rooms, and he knew that a few of them on his floor were empty. He left his own room and moved along the corridor. Selecting a room near the fire escape, he stopped and listened outside. When he couldn't hear anything, he knocked gently on the door. No answer. He quickly picked the lock and stepped inside. The beds were unmade with the blankets stored neatly on the mattresses. It was now twelve-thirty and highly unlikely that they would rent the room that night.

Tomorrow he would know if he had bought enough time.

• TWELVE •

AS DALTON LAY ASLEEP in his borrowed bed, the manhunt began.

Maitland-Jones' body was taken to the city morgue. The gun, the handkerchief, and the contents of his pocket were then taken to the nearest precinct station. The following day his clothes would also be sent to the station. While the body was still on the train, an officer from the Homicide Squad had sorted through the pocket contents. When he located the Consulate identification card he immediately contacted his superior, who in turn contacted the Consulate.

An official was quickly dispatched to the morgue to make a formal identification. The British Consul was informed of the killing at the dinner party at which the Prime Minister was the guest of honor.

The Consul hurriedly left the party with as little fuss as possible. He was briefed on the details of the killing on the way to the consular offices.

On arrival, he immediately contacted the Mayor. He stressed the delicacy of the situation and emphasized the need for discretion in the investigation. Too much publicity for the incident would not be welcome at the present time.

The Mayor contacted the Police Commissioner. As a foreign attaché was involved, he routinely notified the FBI. A senior FBI agent was quickly dispatched to the Consulate to work in conjunction with the police.

What did you call a Consul? agent Carl Roeder wondered. Your Excellency? No, that was an Ambassador. He considered his reply to the Consul's question. Play it safe.

"No, sir. We're certain that it's not just an ordinary killing. Robbery is definitely out as a motive."

Before he had come to the Consulate, Roeder had contacted the police station to obtain the brief details of the killing. He explained to the Consul.

"You see, sir, all of the witnesses—and we have quite a few—confirm that your man was chased for some distance before being shot. He was obviously trying to escape from his killer."

"Terrible, terrible," murmured the Consul, genuinely shocked.

"Could you please tell me his exact position at the Consulate?" the agent inquired.

The Consul hesitated for a second.

"I trust that anything I tell you will be in complete confidence?" he asked anxiously.

"As long as it doesn't have to be revealed, it won't be," Roeder promised. "But I must emphasize that it is a murder investigation with the New York Police Department involved. . . . "

The Consul pondered the somewhat ambiguous reply and then continued with a sigh. He briefly told the FBI agent of the Consulate leaks and Maitland-Jones' investigation.

"Thank you, your Excell . . . eh, sir," Roeder corrected quickly. "I would like to talk to someone who can brief me thoroughly on Maitland-Jones' investigations to date."

The Consul picked up a telephone and dialed.

" . . . yes, I know it's one A.M., but get around here immediately," he said authoritatively.

"Roger Mills," he explained to Roeder with a nod at the phone. "He was working directly under Maitland-Jones."

"Fine," replied Roeder. "While he's coming I'd like to have a look at the victim's office. Incidentally, I assume he had a secretary?"

"Yes, Miss Turnbull."

The agent nodded. "I'd also like to see her as soon as possible. Could you please call her and we'll arrange transport over here immediately?"

"Yes, of course," said the Consul. As he reached for the phone his voice was worried. "What exactly do you think is going on?"

Roeder spoke earnestly. "Sir, we have the murder of a security officer here at a time when he was investigating the leakage of information from the Consulate. The British Prime Minister is in this city at present. A man was arrested in New York today with a rifle and a record of terrorist activity in Ireland. I don't know what's going on, but I want to find out as quickly as possible."

Carl Roeder sat down at Maitland-Jones' desk. He noted the bulky envelope and the sheets of paper that lay on the surface. A quick check showed that three of the lower drawers were locked.

He turned his attention to the sheets of paper on the top of the desk. Briefly, he skimmed through the Duffy police report and the report from London on the man's terrorist activities in Ireland. He then picked up the bulky envelope and removed its contents. Having seen enough surveillance reports, he was able to immediately recognize them as such. The time at the top of the reports showed that they had been completed and signed at nine-fifteen that night.

He had just commenced reading when he was interrupted by a knock at the door.

The young man who entered introduced himself. "Roger Mills. Agent Roeder, I presume?"

Thirtyish, he pronounced Roeder's name with clipped precision.

"Carl Roeder," confirmed Roeder, shaking hands perfunctorily.

"Tell me how far you've got in your investigations into the suspected leaks," he asked brusquely.

Mills wasn't in the least disconcerted. Quickly and succinctly he briefed the agent on the situation to date.

Roeder was agreeably impressed. The Oxbridge accent grated on his Brooklyn ears, but the fellow knew what he was talking about. As apparently did his boss, Maitland-Jones.

"So you reckon it's the fairy?" he asked directly.

"Yes," replied Mills. Uncouth fellow, he thought to himself.

They were both interrupted by the opening of the outside office door. A few seconds later Astrid Turnbull knocked at their door. When she came into the room her eyes were red-rimmed.

Roeder introduced himself.

"Poor Mister Maitland-Jones. Such a nice man," offered his secretary as an obituary.

Roeder picked up the envelope containing that night's surveillance reports.

"You brought this in to him?" he asked kindly.

"Yes," she replied, visibly trying to collect herself.

"About what time would that have been, Miss Turnbell?"

"Bull," she corrected.

"I beg your pardon," said Roeder, startled.

"It's Turn . . . *bull.*"

"My apologies Miss, eh, Turnbull."

He glanced at Roger Mills. The bastard was actually smirking!

"What time did you bring in the envelope?" he repeated, a little harsher than he meant.

"At nine-forty. He signed for it."

Roeder nodded. "What time did he leave?"

"About ten minutes later. He just ran out. He seemed in such a hurry. Most unlike him. He always used to take his time. Such a precise man."

"Just one last thing, Miss Turnbull," said Roeder. "Did anybody contact him tonight? In particular, just before he rushed out?"

"No, nobody contacted him, but he did make a phone call himself."

"Whom did he phone?" asked Roeder quickly. "It could be very important, Miss Turnbull."

"I'm afraid I can't tell you that. You see, he used one of the special phones. It doesn't go through the usual exchange, so I didn't dial the number for him."

Roeder looked questioningly at Roger Mills.

Mills shrugged. "He could have rung quite a number of people on that phone."

"It's a sort of hot line, right?"

Mills nodded.

"Okay. Write me out a list of the people cleared to use it." He turned to the woman. "Thank you, Miss Turnbull," he said kindly. "You've been very helpful. The car will bring you back home now."

"Poor Mister Maitland-Jones, such a nice man," she sobbed as she left.

Roeder turned quickly to Mills.

"Can you open those drawers?" he asked, nodding at the desk.

Mills produced some keys and opened the drawers.

Two of them contained previous intelligence reports and the other one the files on the various Consulate members.

Roeder sat down at the desk.

Okay, something made the guy rush off in a hurry. First of all, he received a sealed surveillance report. Minutes later he made a short phone call, and immediately after that he was off.

Roeder studied that night's surveillance sheets. It didn't take him long to find the part that had caused Maitland-Jones to lose his life.

"This must be what made him run out. He had to be in Greenwich Village by ten o'clock tonight. What information do you have on this woman, Mrs., eh, . . . Helen Taverne?"

"She had full security clearance," Mills informed him. "Nothing so far to connect her with the leaks."

"Well, there sure is now," said Roeder grimly.

He thought for a moment.

"Your visual surveillance. Would it be the same man on now as was there earlier tonight?"

Mills checked his watch. "Yes, the same one."

"Can you contact him immediately?"

Mills picked up the special telephone on the desk and dialed.

The man confirmed that Mrs. Taverne was back home again. He also confirmed that Maitland-Jones had rung him at the time in question.

"Let's go," commanded Roeder.

Outside the Taverne apartment, Roeder spoke again to the surveillance man.

"Mrs. Taverne came back at five after eleven," the man informed him. "Mr. Taverne hasn't returned yet." He was still obviously shocked at the news of his superior's death.

The apartment was on a large block. The building had security doors that could only be opened with a key or an electronic buzzer in each apartment. Roeder ignored the Taverne's buzzer but pressed the building superintendent's instead.

One minute and four buzzes later, a sleepy figure swaddled in a dressing gown appeared at the door.

"Whaddya want?" he snarled, annoyed at the interruption to his sleep.

Roeder showed him his FBI identification and the man reluctantly opened the entrance door. Roeder pushed by him with Mills following close behind.

They got the elevator to the fifth floor, and seconds later rang the bell of the Taverne apartment. Roeder pressed his ear against the door. He could hear voices inside. He rang twice more but there was still no answer. He pounded his fist on the door. It remained firmly shut.

"Get me the pass key from the superintendent," he shouted at Mills.

Mills obeyed immediately. He found himself obeying Carl Roeder without question.

Shortly afterward he returned with the key and they entered the apartment. The television set was blaring away in the lounge.

They found Helen Taverne's body hanging from the steel shower rail in the bathroom. She had secured her wrists in front with a scarf before kicking the stool away. Her feet were only eight inches off the ground.

The hastily scribbled note in the bedroom avowed her love for her husband and begged his forgiveness.

• THIRTEEN •

CARL ROEDER RETURNED to his office. Although it was now three-thirty A.M., there was still plenty of activity in the FBI building. He knew that he would get no sleep that night. He ordered a pot of strong black coffee and sat down to think. He had brought the final surveillance sheet and the police report on the Duffy arrest with him; also the report on Duffy from London.

Okay, what had he got? He did what he always did when starting an investigation—he wrote down the relevant points on a sheet of paper, carefully numbering them as he wrote.

One. Maitland-Jones, specifically assigned to British Consulate from security duties in Ireland, killed while investigating the leakage of information to Irish groups in America. This information not considered to be of vital importance.

Two. Apparent source of this leak hangs herself after arranging to meet an unknown caller in Greenwich Village. Maitland-Jones killed after obviously going to that meeting.

Three. On Maitland-Jones' desk is a file on an Irish terrorist arrested that day in New York as a result of a tip originating in Ireland. Man armed with high-velocity rifle.

Four. British Prime Minister in America.

Roeder tried to place himself in Maitland-Jones' position. The security officer had commenced his investigations into the leaks seven weeks ago. Helen Taverne's husband had access to the relevant information and the Taverne phone was one of several that had been bugged. The wiretaps or visual surveillance had not revealed anything to date. Therefore, if the source of the leak was still passing information during this period, it was not by telephone, or at least not by private telephone. According to Roger Mills, Maitland-Jones' main suspect was a homosexual attaché in the Consulate. Until tonight. The latest surveillance report had obviously made him suspicious of Mrs. Taverne. After reading that report, he had rushed out of his office. He must have been very anxious to reach the meeting place in time.

He arrived and saw or heard something that made it imperative to his killer that he be silenced. His killer chased him and killed him, and was prepared to kill him in an open area with plenty of witnesses in order to insure his silence. Why was it so important to the killer? This was what worried Roeder. After all, the information that had been leaked up to this point wasn't very important. If Mrs. Taverne were exposed as the source, all it meant was the loss of any more such information. Hardly worth killing for.

Roeder shook his head. By the same token, why did she take her own life? After returning to her apartment from her appointment with the unknown man in Greenwich Village, had she killed herself immediately? He wouldn't know until the autopsy report gave the exact time of death. He remembered the television set had been on in the apartment when he and Mills had arrived. Of course, she could have left it on before going out but that was unlikely. No, much more probable that she had switched it on when she returned. Why? A person intent on suicide isn't likely to want to see a late movie. To distract her mind perhaps? Had she seen something on the television that prompted her to take her own life?

Roeder knew that a police statement on the killing had been released at eleven-fifty P.M. The TV channels would have carried it in their late bulletins. She might have seen it and obviously guessed what had happened.

The agent lit a cigarette and sat back in his chair.

He directed his thoughts to Jim Duffy. The man had been questioned intensely since his arrest. As might be expected, he wasn't exactly cooperative. The intelligence report on him from London showed that he was an extremely dangerous young man.

The hotel he had used had been prebooked and prepaid. By whom? The hotel staff couldn't help there. It had all been arranged by telephone and mail. The reception clerk had told them that Duffy had received a telephone call shortly before his arrest. Also that a taxi driver had left an envelope for him that afternoon.

Who was helping him? Directing him? The obvious answer was sympathetic Irish-Americans. Well, Duffy hadn't lasted very long.

Somebody had talked in Ireland and that was that.

After the recent warning that the CIA had received from British Intelligence about a possible assassination attempt on the Prime Minister, everyone had been very relieved to pick up the potential assassin so soon. The man was caught cold. Case closed.

If it hadn't been for tonight's events. . . .

Roeder sat and wondered.

Ten minutes later he picked up the telephone and dialed a number.

The person at the other end had obviously just been awakened, but displayed no annoyance at the fact. It seemed as if he were well used to it.

Roeder spoke to his superior. He synopsized the night's events and included some of his own observations. His superior listened without comment until he had finished.

"What do you want, Carl?" he asked.

"Top priority. Full and immediate access to all our resources. I think we've got to move very quickly."

"Your conclusions?" his superior asked.

"I'm not certain, sir. But with the Prime Minister here we've got to assume the worst."

"Your conclusions, Carl?" his superior insisted.

Roeder breathed deeply. "In my opinion, Duffy could have been a blind. Maitland-Jones guessed this. How, I don't know. The killer had to silence him, and risked chasing him nearly half a mile in the open to do it. Why Mrs. Taverne took her own life, again I don't know. Remorse or fear maybe, take your pick. We've got to assume that she did meet the killer and gave him some information. In view of the fact that the killer went to such great lengths to silence Maitland-Jones, I would assume that the information is far more important than that which has been leaked to date."

He paused reflectively. His voice was worried.

"I think that somewhere out there we've got a potential assassin and I don't think we've got much time to find him."

When Roeder had finished briefing his superior he set about organizing the vast resources that were now at his disposal. The fact that it was four-thirty A.M. was not of significance.

His superior was also busy, making the necessary phone calls to obtain the priority that Roeder had requested. Roeder had sounded very worried. Ever since British Intelligence had informed them that a hit might be on, he had been assigned to cover the British visit until the Prime Minister had returned safely home. All the latest CIA intelligence on the Irish situation had been made available to the FBI.

FBI and CIA cooperation was far better these days than in the recent past. The element of jealousy was still there but it was considerably less paranoiac than before. While the Prime Minister was in America, the FBI would handle his security in close coordination with the latest CIA briefings from Langley.

Roeder gave his instructions quickly.

The murder weapon was collected from the police station and brought to the FBI ballistics department for testing. All of the witnesses' statements were also turned over to the FBI.

Two agents with supplies to do a composite sketch were dispatched to the hospital where the transit cop had been taken. He was lying heavily sedated because of the pain of his fractured kneecap. They would wait at the hospital until he was able to give them what they wanted. Agents were also sent to other witnesses' houses to obtain sketches.

The staff of the Greenwich Village pizza parlor were raised from their beds and shown photographs of William Maitland-Jones and Helen Taverne. A rough composite sketch of the unknown killer was also shown to them. Nobody could remember having seen any of the three faces that night.

A computer trace was started on the Armalite rifle that had been found in the hotel room where Jim Duffy was arrested. This was quickly identified as part of a consignment of ten guns stolen from a gun store in Buffalo five months previously.

British Intelligence was contacted and the American fears made known to them. As a result, scores of people were rounded up in Ireland and questioned.

Roeder waited for the break to come. At five-thirty he stretched out on a couch that had seen similar use in the past. Before he went to sleep, he left strict instructions that he was to be awakened immediately if anything happened. One way or another he was to be up no later than seven A.M.

At seven A.M. precisely, he was called. He splashed ice-cold water on his face and returned to his desk. He contacted the ballistics department and requested a preliminary report. The ballistics officer told him that the murder weapon was a .44 Magnum, with the serial numbers filed off. The filed area had apparently been etched with acid to insure that the gun was untraceable.

"Can you give me anything that might be of help?" Roeder asked him. He could almost see the man shrugging.

"Well, the two bullets we got from the body were definitely fired from this gun."

"No kidding," said Roeder sarcastically.

"The other bullet, the one that smashed the window, was completely flattened as it carried through and hit a steel grid. There's just one other thing. This gun has fired five bullets, not three. But it's impossible to tell when the other shots were fired."

Roeder hung up.

The last item was interesting. When had the other bullets been fired? There was no report of the man shooting before he reached the subway station. It was a thin straw but it might be worth following up. He ordered a computer check of all .44 shootings in the New York area in the past month.

At seven-thirty the transit cop woke up. Despite the protestations of the doctors and nurses he was persuaded to help make a composite sketch of the killer. An earlier composite based on the other witnesses' descriptions had been rushed to the print rooms of the morning papers. They would be carried on the front page of the early editions.

Of the seven composites, including the transit cop's, that were finally made up, four of them were reasonably similar, one slightly different, and two completely different. Roeder noticed wryly that the transit cop's was one of those that was completely different. To be fair, the man was probably still dopey.

At eight thirty-five the first break came.

British Intelligence reported that they had traced seven of the other Armalite rifles stolen from the gun store in Buffalo. They had been discovered in Southampton, England, three months previously, aboard a French merchant vessel en route from New York to Cherbourg. While the vessel was in Southampton picking up a new generator, a customs officer making a routine check had casually asked a crew member to remove the lid of a wooden crate. His cursory glance inside had revealed the presence of the deadly cargo.

The captain and crew were arrested and later one of the crew had confessed. The ship had been allowed to sail out minus the guns and the sailor. He was at present serving five years for the illegal importation of arms.

The report continued: "Further interrogation of the sailor, who was encouraged to cooperate by the prospect of a lighter sentence, revealed that he had been approached in a New York bar and offered five hundred dollars to get the guns to Cherbourg. Half before and half after delivery. He said that the name of the man who contacted him was Danny. He was told to go to another bar on Second Avenue for instructions. Danny seemed to be known in this bar. Here, the sailor was briefed on what he was to do in Cherbourg. Apparently, they didn't expect any trouble with customs there. This Danny gave him the impression that a fix was in with one of the customs people."

The report concluded that from their own sources they knew that the owner of this bar was a well-known figure in those Irish-American organizations which raised funds for the terrorists in Ireland. His name was Dominic Lynch.

At eight forty-seven the bar on Second Avenue was raided, and the staff brought in for questioning. The owner wasn't there. He was sound asleep in his home in the Bronx.

Dominic Lynch was awakened abruptly at two minutes after nine in the morning.

• FOURTEEN •

KEVIN DALTON HAD BEEN UP since six-thirty that morning.

He neatly smoothed down the bed and left the room as he had found it the night before. He slipped back along the corridor to his own room and listened carefully at the door. Once inside, he quickly collected a bulky laundry bag and returned down the corridor to one of the bathrooms. Locking the door, he set about his task.

He laid a towel over the sink. From his bag he obtained a pair of sharp scissors and started to snip his hair with the aid of a large hand mirror. He cut it as short as possible, front and back. When he was satisfied, he took a barber's electric razor and carefully shaved the back of his neck. He then rolled up the masses of hair in the towel and stuffed it into a plastic shopping bag.

Next he concentrated on his beard. He trimmed it as much as possible with the scissors and then shaved with an open razor. He took his time, trying to avoid nicking himself. When he was clean-shaven, he washed the sink until it was spotlessly clean.

From the bag, he removed a false beard and tried it on. It was reasonably similar to his own beard in style and color. As he pulled it off again, the adhesive of the fitting surface made his recently shaven face tingle painfully for a few seconds. He returned the false beard to the bag.

Finally, he removed some thin-rimmed spectacles from their case and fitted them on. The lenses were of plain glass.

He studied himself critically in the mirror. His skin was only lightly tanned and felt quite smooth. He looked much younger without the beard.

Leaving the bathroom he returned to his room. Once inside, he immediately pulled back the bedclothes and rumpled the sheets. Unstrapping his watch, he laid it on the bedside locker, along with fifty dollars and some loose change.

He then quickly dressed in faded jeans, checked shirt, and sneakers. Anything that might be of interest he removed from the pockets of his other clothes. He was especially careful to remove the film which he had taken on the helicopter the previous day. He left everything in the room except for the plastic bag with the hair and another small bag with some items which he would require later.

At the doorway he gave one last searching look around, and then firmly closed the door.

Downstairs in the lobby, he joined a group of people heading for the coffee shop attached to the hotel. Its side entrance was just off the lobby. Although it was only seven twenty-five A.M., the midtown hotel was already busy. He quickly walked through the coffee shop and out the front entrance into the street.

Six blocks away, he dumped the plastic bag into a refuse container outside a restaurant. He then purchased the daily papers, entered a nearby coffee shop and ordered breakfast. As he ate he studied the composite sketch and accompanying description on the front page.

Obviously they had moved fast. The composite was reasonably accurate, but they had given too much emphasis to the hair. It made him look wild and unkempt. To the witnesses' eyes, he had obviously appeared as a crazy figure charging along with a gun. There was little resemblance between the untidy, wild-eyed face in the sketch and the neatly groomed, close-cropped young man quietly eating his breakfast in the coffee shop. The gun and the beard had monopolized the witnesses' attention. He noticed that they had made him two inches taller in the description.

The newspaper report gave brief details of the shooting and concluded, "Police are anxious to arrest the killer as quickly as possible. They believe he could kill again without provocation."

They hadn't overplayed it. Perhaps they weren't quite sure of the significance of Maitland-Jones' killing, or perhaps the British had asked them to keep it low-key. Bad publicity from their point of view. There was no mention of the victim being attached to the British Consulate.

The fact that it was front-paged so quickly obviously meant that they knew it was far more than just an ordinary killing. From now on, he was a marked man in New York.

He left the coffee shop and passed the time in two other coffee shops while waiting for the stores to open. At five minutes after nine he bought a new wristwatch in a nearby camera store. In the men's section of a large department store, he bought a light polyester raincoat, a pre-tailored dark blue suit, and various accessories. A light sleeping bag, a new travel bag, and a slim double-clasped briefcase completed his shopping.

He stored all of his purchases in the travel bag.

He had made his preliminary decision over breakfast. The helicopter hit was still feasible. He checked his watch. Nine fifty-seven A.M. The speech at the Statue of Liberty was due for eleven-thirty that morning.

He found a pay phone and rang the helicopter pad. Immediately, he was put through to Angelo Resinelli.

"Angelo? Alan Green here. I'm afraid I'll be a bit delayed," he said mournfully. "My boy's been sick during the night—some kind of stomach bug. Our doctor's coming right over, so I'm waiting until he arrives. But I'll definitely be down later."

"Sorry to hear about your boy," said Resinelli genuinely. "You've booked me for the morning, so I'll be here till you show up."

Dalton talked for a few more seconds and then rang off. Unless Resinelli was a good actor, he was reasonably sure that the man either hadn't read the morning paper or, if he had, hadn't connected it with his previous day's passenger.

He caught a cab to Penn Station and hurried to the locker area. Here he quickly removed the carry-all containing the tested Armalite from the locker and rolled it up in the sleeping bag. He replaced the new travel bag in the locker and walked away. Outside the station he caught another cab.

It was time.

• FIFTEEN •

DOMINIC LYNCH MADE a very specific suggestion to his interrogator.

The experienced FBI agent looked at him without changing his expression. The anatomical difficulties of Lynch's recommendations were considerable.

"Look at the facts," his interrogator went on reasonably. "An Irishman arrested in New York with a gun that was stolen from a gun shop in Buffalo. Most of the batch from which that gun came was shipped out of America. The smuggling operation was planned in your bar. We know you've been involved in the Irish troubles for a long time. Your bar is decorated with anti-British posters. Where's Danny?" he finished abruptly.

"Who's Danny?" asked Lynch innocently.

"Oh, you don't know," continued the agent sarcastically. He walked behind Lynch. "Well, let me tell you. Danny's a man that we want to meet. He's well-known in your bar, and he's definitely implicated in the stolen weapons. You see, there's a little arithmetical problem that we'd like Danny to solve.

"We know how many guns were stolen. We know how many of those were found aboard a ship in England. We also know that one was found yesterday afternoon on a man we arrested in New York. But what we'd really like to know is where the other two guns in the batch are. We're sure Danny could help us." He walked around to the front again and looked directly at Lynch.

"You know something else, mister. We have a pretty good idea that you could help us too."

Lynch looked up at his questioner and calmly repeated his earlier suggestion.

Dominic Lynch was a determined man. His determination had not wavered over the years. He was now in his early seventies but could easily have passed for a man in his fifties. He had lived a dedicated and, at least in his youth, a highly dangerous life. For over forty years now he had been an American citizen.

Born the eldest of six children in a small farmhouse in Cork, his remaining childhood memories were mostly of people hiding. His father was active in the local flying column at the time. Dominic rarely remembered him staying at home more than one night in succession. Often the "Tans" would come and search the house, usually during the early hours of the night and morning. He couldn't understand the remarks they made to his mother, but knew by her reaction that they infuriated her.

On one particular night he had seen a soldier trying to touch her. He could still remember the man's agonized face as he clutched his groin where her sharp knee had buried itself. He thought that they would harm her and had rushed to her defense, his small hands beating helplessly against their uniforms. One of them cuffed him painfully on the head and he and the other children were then locked in a bedroom at the back of the house.

He heard his mother's screams and beat helplessly on the door. When his efforts had no effect, he dropped fifteen feet to the ground from the window and ran half a mile to a neighboring farm. There he sobbed out his story to the sympathetic listeners. A message was quickly passed to his father who was sleeping in a safe house less than a mile away. The other people tried in vain to dissuade his father from rushing off to the family home.

The kind neighbors soothed young Dominic and put him to bed. Despite his tender years he knew that something was terribly wrong. His tears had streaked the pillow before he finally fell into an exhausted sleep.

The next morning the boy slipped quietly out of the neighbor's house while everyone was asleep. He returned to his own home. As he approached he saw the soldiers' large Crossley Tenders parked outside. Army personnel were moving in and out of the front door.

On the ground nearby lay five figures covered with sheets. Three of them had heavy army boots. The others were the bodies of his father and mother.

A kindly army orderly eventually succeeded in pulling the boy away from his mother's body.

Dominic was almost ten years old when his father and mother were killed. With their deaths, the only home that he had ever known was taken from him. The young family was split up. In the Ireland of 1920, most families were hard-put to support themselves, let alone take in six more children. The two youngest ones went to live with relatives in Dublin. Another two were adopted by different relatives in England. Dominic and the eldest girl went to live with their father's sister in County Kerry.

This household was as strongly Republican as his own had been. His aunt, with the exception of that one subject, was a kind and tolerant woman. She tried to treat the two orphans exactly the same as her own children.

Again men came and went at all hours. As he grew older Dominic sometimes bicycled to different localities, carrying verbal messages to the Volunteers. He learned to wave at the soldiers passing by in their lorries as he carried information that could cost them their lives.

When the Anglo-Irish peace treaty negotiations eventually commenced, a wave of euphoria swept the country.

News came from London of the signing of the treaty and the partition of the country into the Irish Free State in the south and the separate British state of Northern Ireland in the north. The reaction in some households was total disbelief. The apparent compromise so negated the terrible sacrifices of the previous years as to make a mockery of their long struggle.

The majority of people were glad that at least they'd won something. They were consoled by the fact that the fighting was over, and viewed the partition of the country as a temporary measure dictated by expediency.

The polarization in the south was swift. On one side were those who accepted the treaty, the Free Staters or "Regulars"; on the other were those who felt that dividing the country was a sell-out, the "Irregulars." Three months after the signing of the treaty, hostilities commenced between them. The Irish Civil War had begun.

In Dominic's house the decision to sign the treaty was never accepted. As he grew older, his adolescence was spent as his childhood had been. Only this time the soldiers who came to search the house were Regulars of the Irish Free State Army.

As time passed, most people came to accept that the struggle was hopeless. The number of Irregulars began to dwindle and their support was gradually eroded. The Free State Army gained total control of the twenty-six counties of the south. The Irregulars were beaten, but there was still a hard-core group who refused to lay down their arms.

As the years went by the bloody memories of the Civil War receded and were replaced by the more mundane problems of economic survival.

Dominic's family never wavered. He became an active member of the Republicans who refused to accept either the treaty or their defeat in the Civil War. He went on the run and was involved in many skirmishes against the authorities on both sides of the border. It was only after two years as a fugitive that he finally conceded the futility of his struggle. He knew that if he remained in Ireland he wouldn't be alive for much longer.

In 1932, he was smuggled onto a ship which sailed out of Cobh harbor for New York.

The sharp instinct for survival, honed by his years on the run, helped the young Dominic in an America gripped by depression. He obtained work in the construction industry and through a combination of hard work and natural intelligence eventually formed his own small construction company. He became a well-known figure in the Irish community in New York. When he sold his construction business he used the proceeds to purchase a large bar on Second Avenue. He was getting older and welcomed the easier pace of life that it afforded him. His bar became a well-known haunt of Irish-Americans and if a young Irishman arrived there without a job he often left with one.

Over the years, Lynch's memories of home began to fade, but he could never bury the bitterness. In the sporadic outbursts of violence in Ireland in the forties and fifties, he helped the "Cause" by providing whatever money and arms he could obtain.

When the violence erupted again at the end of the sixties, Lynch was caught slightly off guard. For over ten years the issue of partition had been a complete non-runner in an Ireland dominated by economic concerns. He responded by helping to organize dinners and raffles, rummage sales, and musical evenings—anything to obtain funds. Collections—to which Irish-Americans contributed generously, at least at first—were held outside churches. But funds from America fell dramatically when the results of indiscriminate bombings were flashed across American television screens.

Lynch was a firm opponent of such activities. The war, in his time, had consisted of ambushes and shoot-outs with military opposition in which the attacker always ran the risk of being killed. He didn't understand these bombings. He forcibly informed the people in Ireland of his views and warned them of the mass alienation of support that was occurring. Despite this, he still remained firmly committed to the ideals of the cause he had served for most of his life.

"Where's Danny?" the agent repeated insistently, looking directly into Dominic Lynch's face.

Lynch looked back at him.

"If you don't mind, sonny, I'd like to call my lawyer now."

The agent stared at him for a few more seconds before turning and walking out of the room. Another agent immediately took his place.

The first agent went to another room where a young man was being held. He was one of the early-shift barmen at Lynch's bar. In some adjacent rooms the other barmen were being questioned.

The agent looked at the barman closely. Young. No more than twenty-one, he estimated.

"Look, son, we have a problem," he said in a kind, almost fatherly way. "All we want to do is to find Danny." He spoke as if he knew who Danny was.

Before the barman could reply the agent abruptly switched the subject.

"How long have you been in the States?" he asked, much less kindly now.

"A year," came the reply.

"Got a Green Card?" asked the agent.

The young man's downward glance told him the answer. So the kid was an illegal alien. He looked too young to have been in America for long. Irish emigration to America had nearly finished in the late fifties and was now only a trickle, mainly of people with trade or professional skills. It was unlikely that this young man would have obtained a permanent visa. Not to work in a bar.

"Where you from, Pat?" The fatherly voice again.

"Galway," the boy replied in a low voice.

"Well, Pat, you'll be heading back there soon, I'm afraid."

The boy nodded miserably. He was not wanted for anything at home. He had just entered America on a visit, liked it, and never left. He had been working at the bar for a year and was very keen to settle in America.

He wasn't involved in the troubles but had often gone to functions organized by his boss, Dominic Lynch. He was aware of what the money raised by these functions was used for but had never asked any questions. He had a well-paid job off the books and knew when to keep his mouth shut.

"On the other hand, I could forget what I've just heard," the friendly voice told him.

The boy's head looked up. He knew what was being asked.

"I just want one thing—to locate Danny," the agent went on earnestly. "Nobody will ever know how we located him," he promised reassuringly.

The boy looked doubtful. Seeing that he was wavering, the agent pressed his arguments forcibly.

"Look son, whether you talk or not we'll soon get him, probably within hours. Do yourself a favor—you walk out of here with the other barmen and nobody's the wiser."

The boy made his decision.

"As far as I know, Danny hasn't been in the bar for the last three days," he finally offered. "I was on the night shift four days ago, and he was in then."

"What's his second name?" asked the agent.

"Danny Moore."

"Where does he live?"

"He's got an apartment in Queens." The barman gave the agent an address.

"But he's not there now," he added, eager to talk and get it over with.

"Oh, how's that?" asked the agent sharply.

"He's in Boston. Gone to stay with his sister. He mentioned that he was going out of town for a while."

"You wouldn't have his sister's address in Boston, I suppose?" asked the agent hopefully.

The barman didn't have it.

Eight minutes later the apartment in Queens was raided with specific instructions. It took six more minutes to find a letter with a Boston address.

At ten fifty-two A.M., Danny Moore was arrested in a small house in South Boston.

• SIXTEEN •

CARL ROEDER WAS very tired now. He had just finished making a preliminary report to his superior. He had asked him about the possibility of the Prime Minister's schedule being altered for the next twenty-four hours. With luck, they would have the man by then. When the suggestion was put to the Prime Minister the answer was a flat no. Roeder hadn't really expected anything else.

At nine thirty-five a message came through of yet another possible identification—the seventeenth since the hunt began. Every one of these had been religiously checked out, no matter how unlikely. One was from a wife who was absolutely convinced that her husband was the "wild-eyed killer."

The latest one was from a hotel in Manhattan. A clerk there thought that one of the guests looked like the man in the paper. An agent was dispatched to check it out.

When he rang back he reported that there was nobody in the room. Some money and personal effects including a watch were still there; likewise the occupant's travel bag and clothes. The bed had apparently been slept in last night.

Doesn't sound like much, thought Roeder. Maybe the occupant had just slipped out for breakfast.

"Just one odd thing," continued the agent. "The clerk told me what made him remember this particular guest. Now, it so happens that he was the same clerk who handled the booking when the guy arrived. Apparently the guy paid his hotel bill completely in advance. Insisted on it. Said something about liking to settle up beforehand. He signed the register as David Robertson, with an address in Pittsburgh."

"So?" asked Roeder.

"Well, the guy spoke to the clerk later that night. He asked to be called at seven-thirty the next morning."

"Get to the point," said Roeder irritably.

"Well, it was the words he used," said the agent. "He asked to be called at half-seven, not seven-thirty. That struck the clerk as a bit odd. He's used to Britishers staying at the hotel. That's what they say when they want to say seven-thirty or whatever—half past the particular hour. He wouldn't have noticed if it hadn't been for the fact that the man seemed so obviously an American and gave a Pittsburgh address."

"Check his luggage," said Roeder quickly.

"I've already done it," the agent replied. "It all seems to be American made and there's a Pan Am sticker on the case."

"Stay in the room. If the man comes back, arrest him. Don't fuck around. If he is who we're looking for, you mightn't get a second chance. Give me that address."

Eight minutes later he had confirmed that the address given by "David Robertson" did not exist. Two more agents were sent down to the hotel. It looked as if the guy might be coming back soon.

Roeder considered. The guy had booked the hotel four nights ago. He had talked like an American. All of his belongings were American. A careful man. Even the slip about the time hadn't been too big. He was a bit unlucky to have found a smart clerk.

At ten-forty the big break came. A possible identification from the East Side Helicopter Terminal.

Kevin Dalton looked out of the cab at the East River. He was moving along FDR Drive exactly parallel with the river. As the cab went past the Island Heliport Terminal, he gave it a quick inspection; just what a casual passerby would do when passing a row of helicopters easily visible from the road.

Looked normal enough.

He ordered the driver to drop him just beyond the New York University Medical Center. When he had paid him off, he walked away from the Heliport Terminal toward First Avenue. Crossing the street, he entered a busy café, the sleeping bag tucked firmly under his arm. He ordered a cup of coffee and sat down. As he drank, his eyes located the men's room just off the dining area. He went inside and gave it a brief look over. No good.

He left quickly and walked along First Avenue, parallel to the

Heliport Terminal, but a block higher up. He found another café where he repeated the procedure. The entrance to the men's room in this café was off a passageway toward the rear of the building. In the passageway he found what he was looking for—a small storage area for mops and cleansers. He went into the toilet, locked himself in a cubicle, and swiftly reassembled and loaded the Armalite. He replaced it in the carry-all, rolled the sleeping bag around it, and walked back into the passageway.

Quickly he opened the door of the mop storage area. If anyone came in he'd have to tell them he was looking for toilet paper. He jammed the sleeping bag and carry-all into the back of the space and threw some of the cleaning rags and mops over them. He knew it was a slight risk but better than walking around with the gun. He didn't anticipate leaving it there for more than a few minutes. If they were on to him, they might question anyone approaching the helicopter pad carrying a bulky item that could conceal a gun.

He checked his watch. Ten forty-two.

He left the café and turned down Thirty-fourth Street toward the river. When he reached FDR Drive, he was now a hundred yards away from the entrance to the helicopter pad. Most of the southbound traffic was heading onto the FDR overpass at this point. He paused at the traffic lights before commencing his walk. He moved slowly, but not conspicuously so, along the other side of the street.

When he was only fifty yards away he saw a car screeching to a halt outside the entrance. Two men got out and rushed inside. He continued his walk, temporarily screened from the pad by the side wall of the overpass. When it was again visible he was twenty yards beyond it. Imaginary eyes burned into his back as he casually paused to watch some students playing platform tennis on a court in the nearby Medical Center. Continuing at a steady pace he finally turned onto Thirtieth Street and headed over toward First Avenue. On First Avenue he found a pay phone and rang the pad.

"Mr. Resinelli, please," he asked pleasantly.

Resinelli came to the phone.

"Hi, Angelo," said Dalton, making himself sound a little breathless. "Alan Green, here. I'm just on my way down. I should be there in about twenty minutes, okay?"

After a few seconds' hesitation Resinelli replied.

"Sure thing, Mr. Green . . . see you then."

"Okay. I'm rushing off now. See you in twenty minutes."

Dalton gently replaced the receiver.

"Good," said the agent to the sweating Resinelli as he took the phone from him. "You did very good, Mr. Resinelli."

"Jesus, what did the guy want with me?" Resinelli asked, his eyes bulging.

The agent didn't bother trying to explain.

"Never mind. You needn't worry now, we'll soon have him."

"He seemed to be such a nice guy," said Resinelli, almost to himself. He hadn't seen the newspaper sketch, but the fair-haired clerk that Dalton had talked to earlier, and who had seen Dalton on the two occasions he came to the terminal, had recognized it and shown it to Resinelli. They had then decided to contact the police.

"Tell me everything the man said to you and everywhere you went on the flight," the agent asked him.

His partner contacted Carl Roeder. Ten minutes later all the streets around the helicopter pad were being kept under discreet surveillance.

Kevin Dalton was in a cab heading across town to Penn Station. He had returned to the café, quickly drunk another cup of coffee, and retrieved the unnoticed carry-all.

Now that he'd been made, his decision was simple. If everything had been clear he would have put on the false beard and corduroy cap in the toilet of the café and returned to the pad. The loss of the handgun when he collided with the fat woman the night before had been awkward, and he would have had to coerce Resinelli with the Armalite. Still, it should have been feasible. Had he completed the hit and landed safely afterward, he would have removed the beard and faded into the subways as planned.

No matter. He'd lost this round. The important thing now was to get out of New York. They would be very confident after this. The more confident, the better. As far as he was concerned, the Prime Minister had only won a short reprieve. His cab arrived at Penn Station.

Forty-five minutes later, Kevin Dalton left New York on the noon train to Washington.

Roeder received the report from the helicopter terminal with something approaching elation. Now they had him! They'd blown his plan.

He quickly checked the Prime Minister's schedule for the day and immediately rang back the Heliport Terminal. He spoke to the agent who was questioning Resinelli.

"Where did the guy go on the helicopter ride yesterday?"

"Well, sir, he visited a large number of sites."

The agent gave a quick description of the flight.

Roeder thanked him and rang off.

It had to be the Statue of Liberty. It was the only public-speaking function planned for the morning.

He contacted the official responsible for overall security for the Prime Minister's stay in New York and inquired about the security arrangements for that morning, specifically at the Statue of Liberty.

He listened silently for a few minutes and then gave brisk orders.

"Double the aerial surveillance. I want army helicopters there as well as police. Nothing, absolutely nothing to be allowed in the airspace around the statue."

After he had hung up, Roeder felt a little more relaxed. He immediately dialed the FBI building in Boston where Danny Moore was being held, and gave specific instructions for Moore's interrogation.

• SEVENTEEN •

DANNY MOORE WASN'T feeling too relaxed. He had drunk too much beer at a singing session in a local Irish club the night before and was feeling the effects today. When they had raided his sister's house, he was fast asleep in bed.

He was somewhat confused and slightly queasy by the time they brought him to the interrogation room.

"We know all about it, Danny—it's blown," the agent started. "We know about the guns and the arms shipment. We know about the helicopter. We know it all."

"What fucking helicopter?" asked Danny, genuinely puzzled.

"We know Duffy was just a blind," continued the agent tonelessly.

"Who's Duffy?" asked Danny, totally confused.

"Let me tell you exactly where you stand," said the agent. "At the least, the very least, we've got you for involvement in stolen firearms. We've also got you for illegally exporting those arms. Unless, of course, you're a registered arms dealer, Danny. Are you a registered arms dealer by any chance?" the man inquired, his voice heavy with sarcasm.

If they had threatened him with violence, he would have reacted. That type of questioning he could understand and cope with.

"But that's only the first course, Danny," the agent continued. "With what Lynch told us we've got you for something much bigger."

"What do you mean 'with what Lynch told you'?" said Danny unsurely.

"He told us everything. All about how you fixed the arms shipment. All about that dumb frog sailor you paid to get the arms to Cherbourg. What was the fee for his services? Oh, yeah, five hundred smackers. But that's small potatoes, Danny. With Lynch's statement we've also got you as an accessory before the fact in a first-degree murder rap."

"Murder? I haven't murdered anybody," said Danny heatedly. "Surely if I murdered anybody I'd know about it," he pointed out with an aggrieved air.

"I didn't say you murdered anybody," said the agent. "I said accessory before the fact. That's the same penalty, Danny."

"It's a fucking lie," said Danny vehemently. "I only delivered the guns to that Frenchie."

The agent kept his face deadpan.

"Persuade me, Danny. I've talked to the man who interrogated Lynch. He tells me that he thinks Lynch is trying to get out of it, trying to lay it on someone else."

"Look, sure I fixed it up with the Frenchie to get the guns over. But I don't know where they came from."

"Lynch says you organized it all."

"Well, he's fucking well lying," insisted Danny. Christ, his stomach was churning over!

"You'll have to do better than that," said the agent, shaking his head grimly. "What did you do with the other guns, the ones that didn't go on the ship?" he asked in a bored voice.

"I just took them to the station like Lynch told me to."

"What about the .44 Magnum? Lynch says you delivered it to the bearded guy personally."

"What bearded guy?" asked Danny again, puzzled.

"Come on, Danny," shouted the agent in an angry voice. "Don't treat me like a dumb fuck!"

"No, look, hold it a minute," said Danny defensively. "I delivered the .44 and the other guns to Grand Central. I didn't meet anybody and Lynch didn't tell me anything."

Just a messenger boy, thought the agent.

"Tell me exactly what you delivered to the station," he asked, a skeptical tone in his voice.

Danny told him. He even remembered the numbers of the lockers in Grand Central Station.

A master key was obtained and the long-empty lockers in the station were opened. It was then eleven fifty-three A.M.

• • •

As the morning passed, Roeder's worry began to return. The guy hadn't turned up at the helicopter pad and he hadn't returned to his hotel room. Okay, maybe he had somehow realized they were on to him. He must be out there on the streets somewhere.

He turned his attention to his inquiry on the .44 shootings in New York. It hadn't drawn anything of interest. There had been a number of shootings in the time-span he had had checked, but in those cases where the bullets had been recovered, ballistics had not matched any of them with those taken from Maitland-Jones' body.

Roeder sat down and thought. He looked at the Telex of Danny Moore's interrogation.

Moore had delivered three carry-alls to Grand Central Station. Roeder looked down the list of what Moore had said was in them.

> three Armalite rifles
> one .44 Magnum (fully loaded)
> one .38 Special (fully loaded)
> a small amount of plastic explosive
> six detonators

"And a fucking partridge in a pear tree," he muttered to himself.

Why so much hardware? Of the original delivery the man still had two rifles and a handgun. And the explosives? Okay, they weren't in his hotel. He was hardly walking around with them all the time.

Roeder picked up the phone.

"I want a watch on all locker areas in every possible public location in Manhattan. Use the cops. Every precinct is to have a composite sketch and description of the suspect pinned to the bulletin board." He thought for a second. "Hold on a minute. . . ."

He dropped the phone on the desk, went into another room, and returned with the carry-all that had been found in Jim Duffy's hotel room. He picked up the phone, quickly described the carry-all, and ordered a photographer to come around. A photo of the carry-all would be circulated to every precinct in the city. Of course, the fellow could easily change bags, but it was just possible that he mightn't.

Roeder sat down again. He returned again to the question of the guns. Again he asked himself, why so many? And why the explosives?

The guy had booked into his hotel four nights ago. Danny Moore had placed the guns in the Grand Central locker three days ago. So the guy only had Maitland-Jones' murder weapon for three days. That narrowed the scope for .44 shootings. What had the man been doing for the last three days? During that time he had apparently fired two .44 bullets.

Roeder picked up the Prime Minister's tour schedule and studied it carefully. No other large public meetings today. A reception with the Governor tonight. Then off to Washington in the morning. After Washington, down to Houston for a day to meet the oilmen and, finally, back home to Britain.

The killer was a meticulous man. His foresight in removing the handkerchief to cover the gun before Maitland-Jones' shooting had impressed Roeder. Obviously the fellow reacted well under pressure.

He looked again at the Prime Minister's schedule and then picked up the phone.

"I want a report on all the .44 Magnum shootings in Washington and Houston in the last three days. Hold it," he continued. "Initially I want a report on just the fatal shootings, but the rest soon after that."

If the killer hit someone with two .44 slugs, that person was most likely dead. Christ, there couldn't be that many shootings in three days, not with .44 Magnums!

In Washington and Houston a computer was quickly programmed to provide the information. In the meantime, Roeder was ordering a check on all rail, coach, and air terminals out of New York. An appeal was made on local radio and TV to all car-rental firms to contact the police if anyone answering the killer's description tried to hire a car, possibly using the name Alan Green or David Robertson.

Thirty minutes after his computer request, Roeder received the Telexed reports of three .44 fatalities in the time specified. Two were in Washington and one in Houston. One was a police killing, which he dismissed. Neither of the other two seemed very helpful.

He contacted the ballistics department. How quickly could they check the bullets of these latter two against the Maitland-Jones murder weapon and bullets?

The ballistics officer was cautious. A lot of care would have to be taken before a positive identification could be made. The gun would have to be fired into a water tank; single shots at first, and then multiple shots in rapid succession to allow for temperature changes as it heated up. All the bullets would then be photographed using micro-photographic techniques. The photographs would be carefully scanned under an electron microscope to check the similarity of the striae. If there was a perfect match, then obviously the bullets were from the same gun. However, even if there were some small differences, it didn't necessarily rule out a match. Sometimes it needed a very experienced ballistics expert to make a decision. If he had a reasonable amount of testing time he would almost certainly make the correct decision, but nobody liked making snap decisions. . . .

Roeder quelled his impatience.

"I don't want a positive identification at the moment. I just want an educated guess."

"In that case, what we'll do is get Washington and Houston to do the electron photography on their bullets and wire the results up to us. We'll then compare them with the bullets we have here, and I should be able to give you your educated guess. But I would much prefer to have the actual bullets themselves."

"They'll be sent up immediately after the Washington and Houston people have done their tests," Roeder assured him, "but get me a preliminary report as quickly as possible."

He spent the time checking the security for the Prime Minister's reception with the Governor that night. With luck, they'd have picked up the man by then.

Seventy minutes later, the preliminary ballistics report was phoned through to him. They thought they had a match, but would need more tests to confirm it. The bullets from the Maitland-Jones killing seemed to match those used in an apparent mugging incident in Washington two nights previously. The victim was an habitual criminal and drug addict.

Roeder digested this information. It would seem to place this man in Washington two nights ago. What was he doing there, besides shooting muggers? The suspicion that had been growing in his mind was chilling.

Maybe the clever bastard had a contingency plan?

He grabbed the phone. "How many planes, trains, and coaches have left for Washington since ten fifty-four this morning?"

That was the time the killer had telephoned the helicopter pad. Perhaps the helicopter pilot had unknowingly communicated something to warn him off?

Roeder received the information six minutes later.

Five flights, four of which had landed. The two o'clock Eastern from La Guardia was still in the air.

Three scheduled coaches.

Eight trains, four of them reserved Metroliners.

None of the coaches or trains had yet arrived. Roeder gave swift instructions.

"Every single passenger flying from New York to Washington is to be checked, and the flight that's still in the air must be caught immediately on arrival in Washington.

"I want all of the trains and coaches boarded at their next stop. Anyone that looks even remotely like our man is to have his luggage searched."

There was nothing else he could do. Now he would just have to wait.

Forty minutes later he was sitting at his desk checking the latest reports when the message arrived. A man had been arrested on a train at Baltimore. In his travel bag was an Armalite rifle. He had tried to resist arrest and had to be forcibly subdued by the arresting officers.

Roeder breathed a long sigh of relief. He immediately arranged for an air force plane to take him to Baltimore.

• EIGHTEEN •

AS THE TRAIN ROLLED through the Maryland countryside, Kevin Dalton stretched his legs in the limited seat space. He was in the fourth carriage from the back and the train was about half full.

When he had arrived at Penn Station, the Armalite had presented him with a dilemma. He had considered the obvious advantage of bringing it with him to Washington. He was vulnerable without a handgun and the Armalite could prove very useful on the journey. However, he had finally decided that the risk of carrying it with him outweighed the advantage of being armed. He would leave it in a locker.

He had entered the station with the carry-all wrapped snugly in the sleeping bag. Down in the locker area he had waited for three minutes before being reasonably satisfied that the lockers were free from surveillance. He then quickly retrieved his travel bag from the locker and shoved the sleeping bag and gun carry-all back inside.

Crossing to the men's toilets, he entered one of the cubicles. Here, he undressed and put on the dark-blue suit and matching accessories that he had bought earlier that morning. He removed the slim briefcase from the travel bag and stuffed his discarded clothes into the bag.

Outside the cubicle he went over to a sink and carefully washed his hands. As he did so, he studied himself in the large mirror over the stand. The suit gave him a more mature look—the rising young executive. He straightened his tie and flicked a small spot of dust from the lapel. Finally, he draped the polyester raincoat over his arm and left the men's room.

He doubted if they would be watching the railway stations already, but decided to assume that they were. The logical place for them to watch would be at the ticket counters or at the gates leading to the platforms.

He walked to one of the ticket counters and joined the small line. After a few minutes he purchased a two-way ticket to Washington. Just as he was turning away, he got the idea. He glanced at the station clock overhead. Eleven thirty-eight. There should be just enough time. He hurried to the platform gates and passed through gate ten. As usual there was no ticket check. Only when the train had left the station would the Amtrak inspectors commence their checking procedure.

An escalator carried him down to the platform two floors below. He entered the second to last coach and hoisted his travel bag and briefcase onto the rack above the seat. Quickly he left the train and walked up one flight of steps to the locker area. Here he retrieved the carry-all with the Armalite and then continued on up to the main concourse. This was the dangerous part. He crossed over to gate ten and again passed down the escalator onto the Washington train. All this time he had kept the carry-all covered with his polyester raincoat. He hoisted it up onto the rack beside the travel bag.

Briefly he checked the time. Eleven forty-three. The whole exercise had taken just five minutes.

He sat down, removed his jacket and tie, and slipped his thin-rimmed spectacles into the breast pocket of his jacket. Again he left the train and passed out shirt-sleeved into the main concourse. At one of the magazine stands he bought some baggage stickers.

The station clock said eleven forty-six. It was going to be tight.

He hurried to the information desk near the ticket counters and leaned against it, apparently studying his timetable. People approached the desk in regular streams with their inquiries.

It took him four minutes to find the mark.

The man he chose was taller than himself, slightly overweight, and casually dressed. Most important of all, he had a full beard. Like a lot of bearded men it was difficult to discern his features. Of course, they could have arranged composites of what he might look like without the beard. Still, first impressions were usually strongest, and a man with a beard would be looked at more closely.

Most people, when traveling, have some sort of identification label on their luggage, and this man was no exception. Dalton made up his mind in a few seconds.

As the man walked away from the information desk toward a

ticket counter, Dalton was behind him. While they stood in line, he had ample time to read the name and address on the baggage label. Luckily, the handwriting was clear and legible.

The bearded man purchased his ticket at eleven fifty-two A.M. and immediately joined the other passengers heading toward the platform gates. Dalton followed at a discreet distance. They passed through gate ten, down the escalator, and onto the platform. The man entered the train between the fourth and fifth rear coaches. Dalton followed after a few seconds but waited in the area between the coaches. He watched the bearded man walk up toward the middle of the fourth coach, select a seat on the track side of the train, and store his luggage overhead.

Dalton waited briefly to make sure that the man didn't move again. Satisfied, he left the train and quickly returned to coach number two. Here he sat down and wrote out three labels.

On the first label he wrote the bearded man's name and address. He had a good mental picture of the handwriting and tried to make it as close as possible. He stuck this label on the carry-all containing the Armalite.

The second label was similar to the first, with the bearded man's name and address. He slipped this label into his pocket.

On the third label he wrote the name Craig Johnson with an address in New York. This one he stuck on his own travel bag.

He hurried from the coach still shirt-sleeved and carrying only the carry-all with the Armalite. It was again partially concealed by his draped raincoat.

He walked down the platform and reentered the train at the fourth coach. In the vestibule he took the second label from his pocket, licked it, and concealed it in the palm of his hand. He then entered the coach and moved casually up the center aisle, carrying the Armalite carry-all still concealed by the raincoat.

Just behind the bearded man, he stopped and casually hoisted the carry-all up onto the luggage rack. As he adjusted it, he firmly pressed the sticky label onto the side of the man's own suitcase.

Unless the fellow actually took the suitcase down, he wouldn't notice either of the fake labels. They were a different brand than the real label, but it wasn't important. People often have different labels on their baggage as relics of previous journeys.

Dalton moved unobtrusively along the aisle past some of the latecomers, who were busy storing their luggage. He walked quickly through the train to the second coach. Here he sat down and slipped on his jacket and tie. A minute later he left the seat carrying his travel bag and briefcase. He stepped out of the train at the third coach, delaying his exit until a group of passengers were passing by. He was wearing his spectacles as he walked down the platform on the outside of this group.

Once again he boarded the train at the fourth coach. He paused briefly in the vestibule and then moved into the coach. He chose a window seat on the platform side, a safe distance behind where the bearded man was unsuspectingly seated.

One minute later the train pulled out of the station.

When he had settled into his seat, Dalton opened a newspaper to the financial section, folded it neatly, and laid it on the vacant seat beside him.

As the train journey progressed, the only people checking the passengers were the Amtrak ticket inspectors. Dalton noticed how much more vigilant they were than their easygoing Irish and British counterparts. If anything was amiss about a passenger they would soon pick it up. When passengers had selected their seats and the train pulled out, the railway conductors moved along the aisles, checking the tickets. Each passenger was then given a seat identification tag which was stuck into a niche above the seat. Passengers were requested to carry this tag with them whenever they left their seats.

Dalton had chosen to make the journey by rail for a number of reasons, mainly negative.

Plane travel had a big advantage of speed but the disadvantage of schedule disruptions and stricter security.

Bus travel was more confining than train travel. Less room to maneuver.

He had considered hiring a car but decided against it. He would be abandoning the car when he reached Washington and an abandoned car could be quickly traced. More important than that, he would need a license to hire the car. He didn't want to use the Alan Green license again. Although he had another two licenses, he preferred not to use them either. They would be needed later. One of them identified him as Craig Johnson, the name he had written on his luggage label.

He had also considered buying a car, but the time element as well as the fact that he would have to abandon it made him decide against it. An abandoned car would lead to a seller and a description. He wanted as few people as possible to see him without the beard.

The idea of stealing a car he had dismissed out of hand. The last thing he wanted was to be pulled up in a hot car by a traffic cop.

He stretched out in his seat and relaxed. The train rode along pleasantly, making the occasional stop at the larger stations. Dalton was left undisturbed by the ticket inspectors, his seat identification tag tucked neatly overhead.

As he sat there, the rhythmic progress of the train recalled another journey to his mind. It was just after his Confirmation, so he must have been about eleven or twelve. His mother was dressed in black and his father was wearing a somber, gray suit. They had caught the early morning train from Kingsbridge for the long journey to Mayo, which had been spent largely in silence. Occasionally, the silence was punctuated by a deep sob from his mother. His father patted her hand and tried to console her, a little self-consciously.

The house would seem so strange without his grandfather. No more leisurely fishing trips or Sunday afternoons in Croke Park, watching the hurling. Even in the last few days of the old man's illness, Kevin had really believed that his grandfather might recover.

On arrival in Castlebar, the Daltons had gone straight to the family home. Various relatives had come from all around the country to attend the funeral. Kevin knew that his grandfather had requested that he be buried in the parish of his birth.

At the graveside he watched as they lowered the coffin into the freshly dug grave. Some of the mourners had military ribbons on their suits, old comrades of his grandfather. Kevin remembered some of the faces from the frequent times they had visited the Dalton home. One particular man he remembered from a visit six months prior to his grandfather's death. On that occasion he had heard the old soldier jokingly call his grandfather a "West-Brit coward." Both men had then laughed as if at some old forgotten joke.

Kevin was curious at the phrase and later that night had asked his father what the man had meant. He was alone with his parents in the kitchen at the time, his grandfather having gone off with the man to some reunion.

His father looked at his mother and then back at Kevin.

"He didn't mean it, Kevin. It was just a joke between them."

"Oh, I know that. I was just wondering."

His father smiled at him. "Well, it's a long time ago now. It's partly to do with that old uniform your grandfather has upstairs."

Kevin nodded. He had seen the khaki uniform hanging in his grandfather's wardrobe. "The British Army one?"

"That's the one," his father replied. "You see, Kevin, at the time your grandfather joined the British Army, he thought it was the right thing to do; the same as thousands of other young men from Ireland. They believed that they were fighting for something right—to give small countries their freedom. By their efforts they helped to win that war.

"Well, your grandfather went away to France as an ordinary soldier. Four years later, he returned to Ireland as a captain, so it's obvious that he was certainly no coward. During the war, he had seen terrible things—whole towns flattened so that nothing but rubble remained, thousands of people maimed and killed. In just one day, twenty thousand people were killed. Can you imagine that, Kevin, in just one day! Well, for four years your grandfather saw all these things."

"Was that in Flanders?" Kevin asked curiously. They had read about it in school.

"That's right. In Flanders. Anyway, when your grandfather came back to Ireland after the war, he had seen things that people who were not out there couldn't possibly imagine. The memories of what he had lived through made him determined to prevent anything similar happening in Ireland. He dreaded a repeat of all the waste. He became what was known as a pacifist."

"A pacifist," repeated Kevin wisely.

"Now, at that time feelings were running pretty high in the country. Anyone that didn't support the fight for independence was regarded with suspicion. In view of your grandfather's rejection of violence and his previous connection with the British Army, he became a prime target for abuse. Hence the 'West British' part of that phrase you heard. Of course, being a pacifist didn't mean that your grandfather hadn't got strong political convictions. He wanted the Irish people to run this country as much as anybody else, in fact more than most of them. But he'd had enough of violence. He felt that times were changing and that our independence would surely come with it."

"But later on he changed his mind. Why was that?" asked Kevin.

His father looked at his mother. How did you explain to an eleven-year-old boy about random killings and burned-out homes?

"Well, when the Black and Tans came, he just changed his mind. Unfortunately, your grandfather was ahead of his time. Pacifism was not a sentiment well regarded by either side in those times. He had to bury his theories and learn to fight again. Which he did with a great degree of success, though that's not the word he'd use. Nobody called him derogatory names after that, except in later years as a joke, when it didn't really matter anymore. . . ."

Dalton's reverie was interrupted by the shuddering of the train as it came to a halt at Baltimore. When it remained motionless for longer than he thought necessary, he was jerked back to total alertness.

He picked up the newspaper at his side and pretended to read it. When the delay had become generally noticeable, he heard a few murmurs of disapproval from the other passengers. A railway conductor passed through the coach saying something about a signal malfunction on the line ahead.

Two minutes later, Dalton heard the door behind him open. He appeared to be engrossed in his newspaper.

"Excuse me, sir, could I see anything that might identify you?"

"Pardon?" said Dalton, looking up with a puzzled frown. He then appeared to notice the FBI identification badge in the man's hand.

"Your identification, sir!" Smiling, with cold eyes.

"Eh, certainly, officer," replied Dalton. He fumbled for his wallet, fished out the Craig Johnson driver's license, and offered it to the agent.

The agent looked at it closely and then stared at Dalton.

When he had had the photograph taken, Dalton was as clean-shaven as he was now.

"Please remove your spectacles, Mister Johnson," the agent requested authoritatively.

Dalton complied. He blinked realistically as he took them off, like a genuinely short-sighted person.

"What's wrong, officer?" he asked, a trace of anxiety in his voice.

"We're just conducting a routine investigation," the agent replied. "Where are you heading for, Mister Johnson?"

"I've got some business in Washington. We manufacture precision medical instruments," he added proudly.

The agent nodded. "Would you please identify your luggage, sir?"

Dalton leaned his body outward and pointed up at his travel bag.

The agent lifted it down and placed it on the seat. "Please open it," he requested.

Dalton looked slightly aggrieved but did as he was asked.

The agent quickly examined the travel bag, closed it up, and replaced it on the luggage rack. He looked hard at Dalton once more, and then his eyes strayed over the briefcase.

Christ, a stupid mistake! The damn briefcase was empty. If the cold-eyed bastard asked him to open it, it would look very fishy. What sort of a businessman would travel with an empty briefcase?

"Gee, wait till I tell my little nephew about this," he enthused loudly. "He's always pretending to be a CIA agent!"

"FBI," replied the agent automatically.

He looked at the smiling figure for a brief second longer. Then he nodded curtly and headed up the train.

Dalton stifled the relief that flowed through him. He leaned back in his seat, the ingratiating grin still plastered on his face.

There were two agents searching the carriage. Probably a few more on the rest of the train. Every male under the age of forty-five was being questioned. The passengers leaned out to look along the corridor as the agents moved past them. Dalton waited until they were parallel with the bearded man before leaning out. He could just see the side of the man's face. When the agent asked him to identify his luggage he did so. It was duly checked and, for a moment, Dalton thought that the agent was going to keep on going. He lifted the man's suitcase back up and was just turning away when his head suddenly swung around again to the luggage rack. Dalton could see him stiffen, even from where he was sitting. The agent caught his partner's eye.

The bearded man was innocently settling down into his seat.

"Is that your luggage, sir?" asked the first agent, his hand resting on the top button of his jacket.

"What?" The bearded man looked up. "No, you've just checked mine," he said irritably.

The agent nodded to his partner who lifted down the carry-all and also the bearded man's suitcase.

The identical labels that Dalton had stuck on stood out clearly on each of them.

"Open it, Bob," he said to his partner, his eyes never leaving the bearded man. His hand was now completely hidden under the left side of his jacket.

The other agent unzipped the carry-all. As he started to lift out the Armalite, the first agent whipped out his gun and leveled it on the bearded man's head.

"Stand up slowly and move out of your seat," he ordered.

"What the . . . " began the man, alarmed at the sight of a gun suddenly pointing at him.

"Out of your seat. Move it," roared the agent.

What happened next wasn't in Dalton's plan.

In his hurry to get to his feet and into the aisle, the bearded man caught his foot on the metal seat support. As he stumbled forward, he instinctively raised his arms to protect himself.

The FBI agent reacted automatically. Stepping back half a pace, he raked the barrel of his gun across the side of the man's head. The man collapsed heavily to the floor, and, within seconds, the agents had his hands handcuffed behind his back.

The unfortunate victim was only semi-conscious as he was dragged from the train.

Dalton watched his departure with the same degree of interest as the rest of the passengers. It would have been better if the gun had remained undetected. He would have just left it on the train. Eventually, they would have found it and traced the unfortunate bearded man wherever he might be by then.

The end result was the same. He had gained valuable breathing space. They would spend precious time before they discovered their mistake. By then he would have commenced his schedule. . . .

Fifty minutes later the train pulled in at Union Station.

Dalton collected his luggage and walked toward the platform exit. The two agents at either side of the exit were giving only token inspections to the stream of passengers. No luggage searches were being carried out. One of the agents had a small radio receiver in his hand. Obviously, the news had come through from Baltimore.

Dalton passed through unchallenged. He felt a surge of confidence as he walked beyond them. He had arrived safely in Washington.

· NINETEEN ·

AS HE RAN from the plane to the waiting car, Roeder tried to forget the fact that he was hungry. He was also very tired, despite having dozed on the flight down to Baltimore.

On the short journey to the building where the suspect was being held, he felt a twinge of curiosity about the man. He had, of course, met many killers in his time, but nearly always criminals motivated by profit. He had also met a few of their own potential political assassins. Almost every single one of these that he'd met had been unbalanced and inept, with an imagined grievance which could somehow be settled by killing some politician. Occasionally they did get close enough to the target, but they rarely succeeded in the attempt, either through good security screening or their own stupidity.

Professional killers would hardly ever accept a political contract because of the subsequent heat.

So after the professional and the nut were eliminated, that left one other category: the fanatic. Like this guy.

Roeder was relieved that they had got him so quickly. The shit would really hit the fan if the Prime Minister arrived in Washington with the assassin still loose. He modestly congratulated himself that routine legwork had produced the results. There was always a large element of luck about an investigation, but Carl Roeder always worked hard on making that luck. As in everything, the harder he worked the luckier he got.

The car rolled to a halt outside a gray, nondescript building. As he stepped out, Roeder turned his collar up against the light drizzle that had greeted him on his arrival in Baltimore. He walked quickly inside the building and went to an elevator. Down in the huge basement, he was brought to the special interrogation section.

The interior of the building contrasted sharply with its drab exterior: bright, painted walls and uniformed men on duty at various exits.

When Roeder entered the room adjacent to where the bearded man was being held, he was met by the two agents who had made the arrest.

The younger one couldn't stop the self-congratulatory smirk.

The older one was more restrained, but still managed to look pleased with himself.

Roeder ignored both of them and walked over to the one-way window.

The bearded man was seated on the single chair in the room, tight-lipped and very pale. A white bandage circled his forehead.

Roeder turned to the older agent. "Okay, fill me in quickly."

The agent nodded at the one-way window. "He keeps insisting that we've made a mistake; that his name is Alvin Bertschin. Address in New York. Says he never saw the carry-all or gun before; says he was going to Washington for a three-day vacation and staying with his brother; says he's going to sue us for false arrest and assault."

Roeder felt a twinge of alarm. Surely the prisoner knew they had enough witnesses to identify him without any problem. What was the point in continuing with the charade?

"Did you check him out?" he asked the agent.

"Not yet. We weren't able to question him for a while. I had to subdue him a little on the train." This, with a certain note of pride.

Roeder walked to a table in the room on which the carry-all and the man's luggage and belongings were neatly placed. The Armalite was laid out beside the carry-all.

Roeder ignored the gun and examined the contents of the wallet.

Driver's license. Letter addressed to Alvin Bertschin. Looked good. A couple of other slips of paper with Alvin Bertschin written on them.

"Get New York to check this address, top priority," he ordered the younger agent. "And get that goddamn smirk off your face!"

He entered the door to the room where the bearded man sat. He had to find out quickly.

Alvin Bertschin looked up hopefully as he came in.

"All right, you dumb fuck, you've had your try," Roeder started. "So you forged some identification—we'll have that proved in half an hour. Where's the other Armalite and thirty-eight that Duffy left in the locker?"

He stood directly in front of the man and lowered his face so that his eyes were just an inch away from Bertschin's. "Where?" he shouted fiercely.

Alvin Bertschin recoiled automatically. His head was aching terribly.

"My name is Alvin Bertschin. I'm from New York, and I don't know what's going on. Oh, Jesus, please believe me."

At that moment Bertschin retched uncontrollably, and a stream of vomit hit Roeder full in the chest. The agent stepped back in disgust and jerked the door wide open. He shouted for somebody to clean up the mess and walked through into the observation room. The empty heavings of Alvin Bertschin followed his ears.

As he stood over the sink and tried to wipe the vomit from his suit, Roeder felt the alarm rising in him. He could still hear Bertschin through the open door. The man was now sobbing away unashamedly.

A cold-blooded killer?

It just didn't fit.

Oh, the bastard! The devious bastard. He'd suckered them! He'd figured them out and played them along. For the first time in the investigation Roeder felt a sense of deep personal enmity toward his quarry.

Twenty-five minutes later the fresh-faced young agent came back, his face now wiped clean of any smirk. New York had checked the address given by Alvin Bertschin. A concerned wife had confirmed his departure to Washington that day.

Roeder received the news with resignation. As a formality, he issued instructions for the helicopter pilot, Resinelli, and two of the witnesses to the shooting in Greenwich Village to be flown to Baltimore. It was obvious that Bertschin was not their man.

He looked down at his now soaking suit. The occasional fleck of undigested food still remained. The young agent was sniffing as if he hadn't quite detected the source of the stench.

Roeder glared at him and stormed out of the room. Somehow he just didn't feel hungry anymore.

• • •

Two hours later Roeder's hunger was back.

He had left Baltimore directly and hurried on to Washington. In the FBI building, less than a mile from the White House, he had enjoyed a quick shower, obtained some reasonably well-fitting clothes, and was eagerly looking forward to the prospect of some food.

Before his hunger could be assuaged, however, he received a telephone call from his superior. It was then seven forty-five P.M. and he had had a total of one and a half hours' sleep since the previous day. As he talked, he still felt wet in his new clothes. He quickly informed his superior of all the developments including the positive elimination of Alvin Bertschin by the witnesses.

His superior listened without comment until Roeder had finished.

"All right, Carl, what do you suggest?"

"National coverage," Roeder replied unhesitatingly. "We've got to assume that this guy is in Washington. We've got to make it so tight for him that he won't be able to show his nose. Get everybody looking for him."

"From his record to date, I'm inclined to agree with you," said his superior in a tone of voice that Roeder knew.

Here it comes, he thought.

"But we can't do it," his superior went on. "I've had my instructions. The whole thing has got to be as low-key as possible. The British feel that the publicity generated by such coverage for one individual would be completely out of proportion to the threat posed by him. They feel that our normal investigative procedures will be enough to get him."

"Nice to have their confidence," muttered Roeder, accepting his investigative handicap resignedly. "Exactly how far can we go?"

"Full cooperation of Washington Police Department, access to all local radio and TV stations, and that's it," his superior informed him. "No mention whatsoever to be made of a possible assassination attempt."

Roeder replied irritably. "Look, they can't have it both ways. If we push hard, the media will tie in the murder hunt, the questioning of the Irish organizations here, and the Prime Minister coming tomorrow. The best we can hope for is a small delay before they add it up. Maybe a few hours. We're already getting a lot of press interest because of the activities in New York today."

"It'll have to be played that way for the present," said his superior crisply. "If we can get him quickly, we're okay. We can deliver the story to them all wrapped up."

"And if we can't?" asked Roeder.

"Then the British will just have to accept the publicity. Better that than taking the chance of the Prime Minister being hit in America."

Roeder sighed. "Okay. We're assuming that the guy is in Washington. Unless, of course, he simply put the rifle on the train, but didn't go himself. I think that's unlikely as he'd be well aware that the longer he stayed in New York, the greater his chances of being picked up. Naturally, we'll keep pushing just as hard for him there. If he's still in New York, the only possible opportunity for him would be at the Governor's reception tonight. It's a small semi-private affair, and I've gone over all the security arrangements. I don't see any way of penetrating them.

"The Prime Minister arrives here in Washington tomorrow morning at twelve-thirty. We've got to assume that our man is going to try for the hit as soon as possible. The longer he waits, the better our chances of getting him. But we can't afford to wait for him to make his move. We've got to get him before twelve-thirty tomorrow. After that, we're on borrowed time."

"What's your feeling, Carl? Surely the guy is wide open now? We're going to make the security so tight in Washington that a hit will be almost impossible."

"Frankly, sir, I don't know about this one," said Roeder doubtfully. "I don't think we should underestimate this man. Up to now he seems to have planned ahead very carefully. The ballistics evidence puts him in Washington two days ago. I think he's working to a well-rehearsed plan. When things have gone wrong with that plan, he's kept his head. That trick on the train was a nice piece of opportunism and shows that he's thinking the way we'd be thinking and staying ahead of us. I just wish we had some more positive identification. Almost everything he's done so far indicates that he's an American. Or so he wants us to think. If we accept this at face value, it means he's either a professional hit man working for money or an Irish-American working from political convictions.

"We have no word of any contract going out. This guy is damn good. If he's a pro, he wouldn't be cheap. A contract like this would carry an enormous fee, and we'd definitely have heard about it. The other thing that tends to rule out a pro is the fact that the guy is using guns obtained from Irish-American sources. A pro would have his own sources.

"If he's a sympathetic Irish-American, he's one that's no stranger to guns. Maybe an ex-serviceman, or even a cop. We're checking the composites against every possible national record. Also every decent print we got in that hotel room in New York."

"What about that expression he used when he asked to be called in the hotel, the half-seven thing?" pointed out his superior. "An Irish-American wouldn't say that."

"No, he wouldn't," agreed Roeder. "But an immigrant might. Especially if he was only in this country for a short time. The immigration people are combing their records for any possibilities. If he's an immigrant he's been here long enough to pass off realistically as a native-born American. Perhaps he still occasionally uses that phrase without even realizing it."

"And if he's not an American?" his superior asked.

"Then he's got to be one of their own men from Ireland, specifically sent over to do the job. Perhaps he's lived in America before. We've told the British and they're doing their damndest to find him for us. Until we get something more definite, we've just got to throw the net out blindly and hope that anything strange will be swept up in it."

"We'll get him," said his superior, his voice full of confidence.

Roeder replaced the receiver in the cradle and thought silently for a few seconds. Suddenly he shouted for one of his assistants. His shout was so fierce that the man burst through the door in a run.

"Mackenzie," he snarled at the new arrival, "this investigation will collapse without some roast beef on rye and a couple of beers."

"Make it Lowenbrau," he shouted at the departing man's back.

That evening, the headquarters of certain Irish organizations in Washington were raided. Known Irish-American fund raisers were picked up for questioning. The federal authorities tried to give the impression that the roundups were just a precaution in view of the Prime Minister's impending visit.

It didn't take long for the allegations of harassment to surface. The news bulletins carried interviews with a number of prominent Irish-Americans protesting what they called the overreactionary measures on the part of the authorities.

Because of the unexpected clampdown and the nature of the questioning, it didn't take long for the Irish groups to figure out that something more important than routine security was at stake. They were puzzled, but tried to hide their bewilderment in a barrage of accusations against the authorities for allegedly "bending to British diplomatic pressure."

Which was just what Roeder expected. The amount of pressure applied had to be carefully gauged. The Prime Minister's visit was contentious enough without further inflammation. FBI agents and police combed the hotels, starting in the vicinity of the spot where the mugger's body had been found the week before.

Television bulletins carried the composite sketch, with a bald message that the man was suspected of recent murders in both New York and Washington. He was believed to be in Washington at present and considered to be armed and dangerous. Hotels and rooming houses were especially advised to be on the lookout for the suspect. No mention was made of his Irish connection.

Underworld contacts were given the word that the man was badly wanted and any worthwhile tip would be well rewarded.

Back in New York, Dominic Lynch was interrogated yet again. He was now beginning to feel the fatigue.

Well, so what. He was an old man now. They'd be badly disappointed if they thought his age would help them, though. To be fair, they had treated him quite decently since his arrest. They were probing blindly, he knew that.

After he had asked for his lawyer they had allowed him to make the phone call. That stupid prick Donegan was out playing golf and had taken almost two hours to arrive. During that time, they had kept at him with their incessant questioning. The room in which he was held was bleakly functional. Its drab olive-green walls stared back indifferently if his eyes wandered from the interrogators. The sole item of furniture was a wooden chair which he found increasingly uncomfortable.

When his lawyer finally arrived, Lynch was escorted to another room to meet him. The lawyer had insisted that either his client be charged with something specific or immediately released. An agent had promptly charged Lynch with suspected firearms theft, possession of firearms without a permit, and conspiracy to smuggle said firearms out of the country.

"Thanks, Donegan," said Lynch sarcastically. "You're a great help. All that and it's only your first minute here. Ten more minutes of you and I'll be beyond needing help." His smile belied the words. The lawyer was an old friend.

Mike Donegan spoke earnestly. "Dominic, it looks like a bad rap. A federal offense. The most important thing right now is to get you out on bail. Just sit tight while I work on it."

When the lawyer eventually returned, Lynch was brought back to the same room to meet him. Donegan's expression was grave.

"I'm sorry, Dominic. The federal authorities are totally opposed to any bail being granted at this time." He shook his head. "There's something funny going on here, but nobody's saying anything. I'm afraid that it looks like you're going to have to spend tonight in the lock-up. It's not very satisfactory, but right now there's nothing more I can do."

Lynch was resigned. "Thanks anyway, Mike. I know you've done what you could. Don't worry, I'm prepared for something like this. You know how it is with me."

Donegan nodded. "I'd like you to write out a list of anything you need. I'll see that it's brought in to you as soon as possible."

After the lawyer had left, the agents took turns questioning Lynch. As soon as they received any information during the day they tried to spring it on him and force a reaction. Lynch looked interested but added nothing to what they already knew.

One of the agents contacted Roeder in Washington.

"I don't know. The old guy acts like it's all nothing to do with him. I swear when we spring something on him he looks really interested as if he's hearing it for the first time. We told him about the switch on the train and he just laughed. He's either playing us along or he really doesn't know what's going on."

Roeder had received all the known information on Dominic Lynch's early life in Ireland. The Dublin government had known of his American activities for a long time, and it was they who now supplied this information.

"Yeah, well, I've been studying his past history. His life before he came to America was something special." He paused for a second. "Look, let's try something different. Try to get him where it hurts and we'll see if it throws up anything."

Ten minutes later the agent returned to the room.

"Well, Mr. Lynch, I think we're just wasting our time on you."

"I'd say that was fairly true, sonny," Lynch agreed amiably.

"You see, our hands are tied." The agent leaned forward confidentially. "You know if it was up to me I'd beat the living shit out of you till you told me about that dumb Mick who thinks he's going to hit the English guy."

Lynch reacted. "I wouldn't have thought he's been too dumb," he said quickly.

"So you know about him," the agent pounced.

Lynch looked at him pityingly. "Sure I do. You've just been telling me about him."

You slipped a bit there, pops, thought the agent. "Well, you know how it is," he continued. "We've got to watch ourselves when we're questioning people nowadays. Not like the old days."

"Look sonny, there's one up there." Lynch pointed up at the ceiling.

"What . . . ?" The agent involuntarily raised his head.

"On the light. I don't want you to miss your daily wing-pulling just because of me. Oh drat, he's flown away. . . ." Lynch looked at the agent pleasantly.

The agent's expression was blank.

"Yeah, there's really nothing we can do. You know, I was reading a book the other day all about you potato-pickers. Boy, they certainly knew how to handle you guys a few years back. What did they call them, the Black and Blues? No, that wasn't it. Black and Greens? No, that wasn't it either. What the hell was the name, pops?"

"Black and Whites?" suggested Lynch helpfully. So they'd done their homework on him. Well, fuck them for all the good it would do them. . . .

"Black and Tans, that's it. The Black and Tans," the agent went on. "You must have been around then pops. Did you ever see any of those boys?"

"Never even a whisper," Lynch replied. "The only Black and Tan I ever met was in a glass, half Guinness and half beer. You should try it sometime, sonny."

The agent kept his blank expression. "I read that the women there would do anything to stop those guys hurting their men. Mind you, I suppose it wasn't all a burden to them, what with the men always being away from home. I guess a bit of diversion might have been appreciated. What do you think, pops? Maybe they didn't mind at all, eh?"

Five bodies under white sheets. His proud father and mother.

"Maybe they didn't," Lynch replied evenly. Jesus, they must be really stretched if this was the best they could come up with.

The agent stroked his jaw. "Yes, I'm sure that nowadays there's a lot of old fellows over there who'd be interested to know if their fathers had Black and Tan uniforms. I guess they'd be about your age now, pops, eh?"

"Well, sonny, when you reach my age, you don't really have too much interest in that type of thing. Mind you, at your age it would be worthwhile checking, that's if the brothel is still there. Who knows, your father might have had a uniform too. But I don't suppose you'll ever know for sure now, will you?"

The agent looked at the old man.

He got up and left the room.

A minute later another agent came in.

"Well, Mr. Lynch, we've just received some information about you."

"Isn't that interesting," replied Lynch, "and you've only just received it. And what might it be . . . ?"

"For a start, there's the question of the killing of a soldier of the Irish Free State Army in 1931."

"Oh, you must have the wrong fellow there. I was seriously considering entering a religious seminary about then. In the end, I finally decided that I could do more good in this godless country than in my native land. Strangely enough, when I arrived here the vocation suddenly left me. In a moment of revelation I decided to be a builder instead. I like to think that God wanted me to be a builder of bridges rather than a fisher of men."

"I see," said the agent poker-faced. "Yes, I see."

Roeder was informed of the interrogation. He wasn't amused. Lynch hadn't actually told them anything but his very negativeness was informative.

A man that had something to hide didn't make wisecracks like that. Not after hours of questioning and on a very emotional subject. Lynch was too relaxed, too cocky—as if he knew they couldn't get anything from him.

Because it wasn't there?

Roeder shook his head. He was still working in the dark.

Again he waited.

At four forty-five that afternoon, Kevin Dalton had walked out of Union Station. Prior to leaving the station he had entered a cubicle in the men's room, removed his blue suit, and changed to casual dress.

He avoided the cabs outside as he walked away from the station. Twenty minutes later he was on a bus heading out of Washington toward Fredericksburg. The bus left him with a three-quarter-mile walk to where he had tested the guns on his earlier trip. The gun club was much quieter than before.

Entering the foliage, he checked his bearings and quickly located the tree on which he had gouged the knife mark. He climbed up and undid the straps that secured the carry-all and suitcase to its branches.

On the ground again, he removed the small transistor with earphones from the suitcase. He sat down at the base of the tree and checked the stations until he obtained a news report. A mention was made of the Prime Minister's visit the next day but nothing else of specific interest.

By now the authorities would surely have realized that they had arrested the wrong man on the train and would be looking very hard for him.

One hour later, he checked the news bulletins again. Just a small item giving the same description as that in New York, but adding that the suspect was also wanted in connection with a murder in Washington. Anyone with information was asked to contact a certain number or to phone any police station.

In the next few hours he regularly checked the bulletins. The later ones carried the reactions of some Irish-Americans to the alleged harassment by the authorities. The item about the murder suspect and the interviews with the aggrieved citizens were apparently unrelated in the news programs. The press would figure it out soon enough anyway.

He switched off the radio and removed the earphones. Darkness had come quickly with no warning twilight like at home. It was still very warm.

He reviewed his position.

He would not be moving from his present site until the following morning. After that he would go to the killing ground. Once he was there all the security in the world would not prevent the assassination of Charles Douglas.

· TWENTY ·

THE PRIME MINISTER was in a good mood.

Earlier that evening he had attended the reception with Governor Tim Foley. It had gone reasonably well under the circumstances. Foley was in his second term as Governor and was regarded by some as a possible presidential candidate. During the dinner they had both made short speeches but had avoided being in any way contentious. The real talking would come later.

In the past the Governor had been outspokenly critical of the continued violence in Ireland. He had met Douglas' predecessor on a number of occasions and had been enthusiastic about the previous attempt to achieve a settlement. The subsequent impasse had bitterly disappointed him.

After the dinner both men had retired from the main body of guests. In their discussion, Foley had put forward his views in an extremely forthright manner. Douglas had listened politely and then reiterated his own position with equal frankness. Despite their lack of agreement the men had eventually parted on reasonably amicable terms. Although nothing tangible had been achieved, to Douglas the exercise was basically a goodwill gesture. Tomorrow in Washington was where the important people could be influenced. . . .

Later, in the quietness of his bedroom, the Prime Minister had turned his attention to the red dispatch boxes which had arrived from London that evening. One report in particular interested him. It was related to the proposed capital punishment bill due for Commons debate in five weeks' time. The last attempt to reinstate capital punishment had been decisively rejected some years before he came to power. He had supported its restoration then, and was disappointed though not surprised at its failure.

At that time Members were allowed a free vote on the issue rather than having to vote along party lines. This time it would be different. The Members of his party would be instructed to vote for the bill. With their majority in The House this should theoretically insure an easy passage. The only problem, however, was the rumbling of discontent which had arisen amongst the back-benchers at the removal of their free vote. Several had threatened to defy the Whip and either abstain or vote against the bill.

The report he now studied was a highly confidential survey of the extent of the back-bencher revolt and a projection of the likely result of the bill—it should still be passed but it would be extremely tight.

The report left him with a difficult choice. If he put too much pressure on the dissidents in the coming weeks, it could well lead to a widening of the revolt and a defeat for the bill. On the other hand, it would be extremely bad for party discipline if they were seen to defy him and get away with it. Of course, dissension on such an emotional issue was not unexpected, though he could never quite accept the logic of the anti-hanging lobby. Dubious statistics showing that it did not act as a deterrent failed to impress him.

His own views on the subject stemmed from personal experience. During the war his role as an intelligence officer had required that he attend the execution of an individual convicted of treason. The judgment was clear-cut. The man had been under surveillance for some time and had openly confessed to his activities. He was small-fry really, a naturalized Polish immigrant whom the Germans had conscripted by threatening his family in Cracow. He had seemed almost relieved when he was arrested.

Despite his total lack of sympathy for the man, Douglas had found the execution harrowing. Afterward, it would have been easy for him to reject the concept of capital punishment, but, in fact, the reverse had occurred. The whole sordid business had convinced him that no individual, no matter how valid his excuses, could be allowed to endanger society without the risk of forfeiting his own life.

For Douglas the war had clarified many things. Although he was working in Military Intelligence toward the end, his career had commenced as a young officer in the Royal Navy. His transfer to Intelligence had come as a result of being torpedoed in the Norwegian Sea en route to Murmansk. The U-boat had struck a hundred and fifty miles inside the Artic Circle and Charles Douglas should have been dead when the last ship in the convoy picked him up. Survival time in the icy water was estimated at a maximum of two minutes and he had already lost consciousness when he was hauled aboard a lifeboat. Sheer luck had tossed him near the lifeboat when the ship's magazine had blown.

Three months in a Russian hospital followed by five months in a Devon convalescent home had restored his basic health while leaving him unfit for further active service. The time spent in convalescence could have been frustrating, but he utilized it as productively as possible. He read voraciously, doggedly practiced the physical exercise program outlined for him, and reconstructed his career in his mind. Just before his discharge he was approached by an acquaintance in Military Intelligence. Such talent and determination would not be allowed to go to waste. . . .

After the war, Douglas had resigned from the services and had immediately gone to work in industry. He knew that ultimately his future lay in politics, but first he would make his mark in the world of finance. When he was eventually elected to Parliament as serving Member for an East Sussex constituency, he had become a wealthy man and a respected figure in The City.

In the decades following the war he had watched with growing dismay the advances of creeping socialism. He fumed at the blind policies which encouraged the indolent and effectively punished the real wealth-makers. He warned of the terrible consequences of uncontrolled immigration, which had already started to manifest themselves; huge areas of London and the Midlands now resembled parts of the Indian subcontinent rather than Britain.

His greatest fear was the insidious undermining of the defense forces. Successive financial cutbacks had reduced the capability of the army to a mere shadow of its former self. He spoke of the ever-present Communist threat which must never be underestimated, despite long periods of apparent dormancy.

As he watched the country slip deeper and deeper into the quagmire, his patriotism hardened into an unshakable determination to halt the process of decline. He knew that his chance would come one day. It was for this that he had been plucked from the freezing waters of the Norwegian Sea. . . .

• • •

Just before he retired for the night, Douglas received a briefing on the latest security situation. He was informed that the potential assassin was still at large and believed to be in Washington. The Prime Minister did not dwell on the news for long. The back-bencher revolt was still fresh in his mind and was far more important. He had decided to defer any action on this matter until his return to England. A personal interview with each of the dissidents should be an extremely effective first step. . . .

Carl Roeder looked at the latest report. They had located the hotel which the man had used on his earlier visit to Washington. Unfortunately, there was nothing there to help them. A watch would be kept in the unlikely event he tried to use it again.

Roeder stretched out resignedly on a couch that had been converted into a makeshift bed.

• TWENTY-ONE •

DALTON WAS AWAKENED by the bright sunlight. His untroubled sleep had greatly refreshed him. He breakfasted on a now stale roll, washed down with lukewarm Coke. It would have to do.

Using the battery razor, he shaved very carefully. Satisfied with the smoothness of his chin, he commenced his preparations.

He removed all the items from the carry-all and suitcase that he had hauled down from the tree. Reluctantly, he decided against carrying the .38. An experienced cop could pick it out under his clothes. He quickly checked the Armalite for any leakage, but all the seals were dry. Most of the items, including the Armalite and the .38, he put into the new travel bag he had brought with him from New York. A few select items he transferred to the suitcase. He then stuffed the empty carry-all deep into some bushes.

It was still too early for him to move. He plugged in the earphones and checked the radio stations. The Prime Minister's visit to Washington was now the main news item. This was immediately followed by a report that it was now believed that the authorities were fearful of a possible assassination attempt. The Washington Chief of Detectives and an FBI spokesman both refused to confirm or deny this. However, the intense manhunt for a particular individual coupled with the questioning of numerous Irish-Americans about the whereabouts of this individual, pointed strongly to such possibility. A report, still unconfirmed, that the suspect's victim in New York was attached to the British Consulate there further strengthened this assumption. Security was expected to be greatly intensified for the duration of the Prime Minister's stay in the city.

When it was time for him to leave, Dalton checked the latest news bulletin. Nothing extra had been added to the earlier bulletins. He stored the radio and earphones in the travel bag with the guns and concealed it and the suitcase in the undergrowth. He would collect them later.

He retraced his route to the bus stop three-quarters of a mile away. There were three other people at the stop.

At nine-forty A.M. he boarded a bus. His destination would take him farther south of Washington, to the town of Richmond. He sat back and relaxed for the journey. The bus was nearly full, and nobody paid him any particular attention on the ride down.

An hour and a quarter later, he arrived in Richmond and immediately went to a large used-car dealership. He had carefully considered the choice of transport for this stage. They would probably have traced the car-rental firm he had used in New York and would be on the lookout in Washington. A rented car was therefore out of the question. He would buy one instead.

He entered the car lot and started looking around. After examining a few cars, he eventually settled on an unassuming Ford Pinto. He spent about five minutes checking the car, occasionally nodding to himself. His obvious interest soon attracted a salesman's watchful presence.

After a few minutes of verbal fencing, the man suggested that Dalton might like a test run. Both men got in and after a quick drive around the block they returned to the lot. Dalton seemed quite enthusiastic about the car and expressed an interest in buying it if the price was right. After a short haggle, they agreed on a compromise figure. Dalton left a hundred dollars deposit and gave the salesman a local address. He said that he would go to his bank to withdraw the balance and would return shortly—he wanted to drive the car away when he had paid in full. He knew that they had an insurance department in this dealership and could provide the obligatory insurance without delay.

The time that he was supposed to be at the bank was spent eating a meal at a nearby delicatessen. Before returning to the auto lot he bought some ham sandwiches and Coke to take away.

At five after twelve he was driving out of Richmond in his newly purchased car. He drove back to where he had spent the previous night, retrieved the travel bag and suitcase from the bushes, and then continued on to Washington. On the journey he listened to the latest news reports. He doubted if they would go so far as to put up road blocks.

Not yet anyway.

Roeder had spent an uncomfortable night. His sleep had been disturbed by strange dreams and did little to rejuvenate him. But a ten-minute cold shower and a bacon and eggs breakfast helped make up for the lack of sleep.

His headquarters had a direct link to the police communication center, and any information was instantly relayed to him. When the night's search had proven utterly fruitless, he once again contacted his superior.

"I don't think we should keep the lid on any longer," he started without preamble. "There's nothing more to be gained by secrecy. We haven't got a smell of him and we're no nearer than we were yesterday. The media have a good idea what's going on, but they're still not absolutely certain. The longer we keep stonewalling the surer they'll become. Why not get their complete cooperation now? Maybe we've missed something important, something they could help us on."

"No, not yet," replied his superior. "Let's try it for a little longer. If nothing breaks we'll review it in a few hours."

Roeder hung up wearily. His head had started to throb slightly. He forced himself to think afresh.

All of their efforts to date had produced very little. It appeared that the man was working completely independent of the Irish community in the area. Feelings were running pretty high in that quarter, but even their angry reaction to the intense questioning had revealed nothing but bewilderment. Some pre-emptive security was inevitable with the Prime Minister's visit, but it was the specific questioning that puzzled them.

Had the killer been frightened off?

The thought had occurred to Roeder before, but he hadn't considered it very seriously. They had to assume that the man was still active. He weighed up the evidence now.

First, the affair on the train: not the act of a man who was running scared. The blowing of his plan in New York obviously hadn't affected his nerve. He must have known that the carry-all switch wouldn't throw them for long. It would just draw attention to the fact that he was heading for Washington. Unless that was what he wanted them to think? If he wasn't in Washington, the only other place for an attempted hit was Houston. But the guy must know that the longer it went on, the greater the risks for him. He couldn't afford to wait very long. The discovery of his hotel and the shooting of the mugger showed that he had been in Washington two days prior to the Prime Minister's arrival. In view of his behavior up to now, it was logical to assume that he had planned something in the event of anything going wrong in New York.

The next thing was the interview with Dominic Lynch. It seemed that although Lynch knew that something elaborate was being planned, he was not informed of any of the actual details of that plan. He had just carried out his instructions dutifully. Who had set the operation up? It must have been ordered from Ireland. British Intelligence was working on that side, but Roeder had a feeling that whoever was behind it was not afraid of Lynch being picked up.

Everything pointed to a man who was working to a careful plan. The plan must allow for the fact that a massive manhunt would be in progress. All of the usual sources of aid would put him in danger, unless he had somebody hiding him that the scope of the investigation would miss. He must know that the security around the Prime Minister would be almost impenetrable. This was the worrying part. What had he planned that could elude the manhunt and penetrate the security screen? If he had any sense he'd be trying to get the hell out. Most men would.

Roeder sighed. But not a fanatic.

Or a very confident man . . .

At noon Roeder walked to the open window and inhaled deeply. The noise of a passing jet reminded him that the Prime Minister was due to land in about half an hour. He walked back to his desk and picked up the sheet outlining Douglas' proposed schedule for the day.

Lunch at the British Embassy.

Helicopter ride to White House lawn for official presidential reception that afternoon.

Post-reception trip to Capitol Hill.

State dinner that night.

At least there were no planned walkabouts or public meetings. All of the guests, and even some of the dignitaries, would be very carefully screened. No unauthorized person would get near the Prime Minister. They would transport him very quickly from place to place. The surrounding areas would be combed for a possible sniper, and traffic would be diverted as much as possible. Looked tight enough, anyway.

His phone rang.

They had traced a budget car-rental firm in New York which had lent a car to a man called Alan Green. One of the clerks had seen the composite sketch on TV last night, but had waited until this morning to check the name. The license details were duly investigated and found to be fraudulent. The car had been used for approximately one day and returned. Payment was in cash. The car had since been hired out to another party.

Roeder thought for a moment.

"Okay, trace the car. I want it combed from wheel to wheel. Also check if they have a record of the mileage used. It might tell us something."

Almost immediately after this they had a response from their plea to Washington car-rental firms. A conscientious, or, more probably, bored clerk, intrigued by the regularity of the murder hunt bulletins, had casually flicked through their carefully indexed filing system. Much to his surprise he had found a card bearing the name Alan Green. The clerk who originally handled the booking had just gone to Florida on vacation.

Two agents were hastily dispatched to the firm. They found that this car had also been rehired and was out on the road again. A similar trace was started to locate it.

Roeder now had a good picture of the suspect's movements from the time he had checked into the hotel in New York until the train journey yesterday. But after that it was just a blank. He glanced at his watch. Twelve forty-two. The Prime Minister would have landed by now.

His phone rang yet again.

"What?" he shouted in disbelief. "He's done what?"

The agent at the other end repeated the message. "He's called an impromptu press conference at the airport."

"For Christ's sake, what's he trying to play at? Doesn't he realize the danger he's in?"

Roeder knew that the British Embassy had been besieged by reporters since early morning. The media had their tails up and were pushing hard.

The agent continued. "We tried to dissuade him but he just smiled and told us in very polite language to piss off. He wants a press conference and he's going to have one, and that's all there is to it."

"Seal the conference room," Roeder ordered. "Search everybody, and I mean everybody, that goes in there. Each reporter is to be vouched for by at least two other reporters before he's let near the place. Fuck Douglas. What does he think he's up to?"

"You can see for yourself in a few minutes," said the agent. "He's being carried live on the lunchtime news. . . ."

Just before one P.M. Roeder flicked on the portable TV in his office. A few minutes later, the confident face of Charles Douglas stared out at him. If the man was worried he certainly hid it well. Roeder waited for the inevitable question. It came almost immediately.

"Prime Minister, would you care to comment on the very strong suspicions that the authorities here are fearful of a possible attempt on your life?"

"Have they actually said this?" Douglas asked innocently.

"No. But they have not denied it either."

Another reporter asked forcefully, "Was it an official of the British Consulate who was murdered last night in New York?"

Roeder turned up the volume slightly. He wondered how the Prime Minister could avoid denying this and its obvious implications.

Douglas paused for a few seconds before replying. "Gentlemen, I promise to give you a comprehensive answer to all your questions in just a moment. But first I would like you to bear with me as I have a number of important comments to make."

The reporters fell silent. Douglas continued firmly.

"There has always been a warm and close relationship between my country and the United States of America. I have come here on this short visit to inform you firsthand of the tremendous changes that have occurred in my country over the last few years. You will remember, gentlemen, that it is not so long ago that you Americans were seriously considering sending food parcels across the Atlantic to our strike-torn island."

His smile was ironic.

"Now, of course, the picture has radically changed. Our economy is thriving. Our standard of living is one of the best in Europe, and many of the divisions of the past have thankfully receded. This is almost entirely due to the policies instituted and vigorously pursued by my party. We have accomplished another Industrial Revolution."

He surveyed the assembled press.

"But also, gentlemen, we have restored the respect for law and order which was seriously undermined. Our police force is once again proud and effective, our judiciary unafraid to bring the full rigor of the law on thugs and criminals. Our streets are now safe."

He pointed accusingly at the newsmen. "I am aware that some of you claim that we have infringed on civil liberties. But I ask you this, gentlemen. If my government is such a paragon of reaction, why do the British people consistently vote us well ahead of the opposition in all the opinion polls? My enemies claim that this is not a true guide to the real feelings of the people. They accuse me of arrogance, of failing to respect the rights of those individuals who do not share my visions and hopes for the future. Of course, they quietly accept the benefits of the economic success my government has created, and then feel free to carp and nitpick at the policies that created the climate for these successes to be realized! Surely theirs is the greater arrogance?

"So, gentlemen, I beg you to see the entire package and not just the isolated parts to which your attention has been drawn by these unpatriotic people."

The Prime Minister sipped a glass of water and continued in his usual forthright manner.

"Now, one of the problems my government has had to face is that of terrorism in Ireland. This brings me to your very specific question which I shall now answer. . . ."

The journalists looked up expectantly.

"I wish to confirm that a member of the staff of the British Consulate was callously murdered in New York last night. You already have the horrific details of the killing. Your authorities have advised me that the person believed to be responsible for this atrocity is suspected of another murder here in Washington. The latest information of the authorities is that the criminal may now be in the Washington area. They have also intimated to me their suspicions that this person may have the grandiose objective of removing me from my present mortal state."

Some of the reporters laughed, a little self-consciously.

"However, they are quite confident that this objective is, to say the least, extremely optimistic. At our request they have not made their suspicions public. We are naturally loathe to give these mindless terrorists the publicity that they so desperately crave.

"I think, gentlemen, that this perfectly illustrates what we are trying to overcome in Ireland. There must be no appeasement of these people. I can only pray that anybody watching me today who would contribute either moral or financial support to them would ponder over what kind of people they are supporting."

One of the reporters cut in.

"Will you rearrange any of your engagements in view of the present security risk?"

Douglas raised his eyebrows. "Good heavens no, of course not! If I reacted to every terrorist threat I would never leave 10 Downing Street. We've got quite used to them now, you know. If the terrorists learn that I'm going from London to Liverpool, I automatically get one. Why, I'd feel quite hurt if they forgot me. It shows I'm doing my job."

The newsmen laughed.

Douglas shrugged dismissively. "Now, gentlemen, we've given quite enough time to this. If you've anything else to ask me please hurry up as I'm rather looking forward to a good lunch at the Embassy."

Roeder switched off the television. Despite his anger at the flagrant disregard for security, he had to admit that it was an excellent performance. The Prime Minister had turned the manhunt into a neat political broadcast. He had obviously decided that as the press were now almost certain of an assassination fear, there was nothing further to be gained by secrecy. He had made it all seem very mundane.

Roeder could see how Douglas had earned his reputation as a man to be respected. Well, he was Roeder's responsibility now, and he was going to make damn sure that nothing happened to him while he was in the United States. . . .

At two-thirty the agent's patience was becoming frayed. Lack of sleep and hastily eaten meals were no recipe for relaxation. He found himself snapping ill humoredly at his subordinates.

He had a terrible feeling of helplessness. In an investigation you did everything you could—made all the checks—and then had to sweat it out. If you were lucky the breaks came quickly. If you were lucky.

He made a decision. He could do nothing more where he was.

Quickly, he briefed his superior and organized the action center to deal with any new information in his absence. He would be immediately informed of any developments.

Roeder set off for the White House.

• TWENTY-TWO •

WHEN DALTON ARRIVED on the outskirts of Washington, he headed north along Washington Boulevard, toward the Theodore Roosevelt Bridge. On the other side of the Potomac, he drove to an underground parking lot where he parked as far from the exit ramp as possible. He removed the travel bag with the Armalite from the trunk, but left the suitcase undisturbed. After locking the trunk he firmly taped the car keys under the back wheel arch. No point in carrying them with him and possibly losing them. Without those keys he was a dead man.

He checked the time. Two thirty-two P.M. Right on schedule.

He slipped on a pair of sunglasses and hurried from the parking lot with the travel bag. He walked almost half a mile before stopping at a pay phone. A woman was making a call, so he waited patiently for her to finish.

When she had left, he quickly dialed a number. It was the same number that the news bulletin had asked anyone with information about the murder suspect to phone.

"Washington Police Department," an alert voice answered. The telephone call would be automatically recorded.

Dalton pitched his voice high.

"Listen, the guy you're looking for, you've got to stop him. Jesus, I didn't know what he was planning. I thought he was just to be sheltered for a while. I've got a family, I don't want any of this."

"What's your name, mister?" asked the police officer on the other end of the line.

"You've got to believe me," Dalton went on unheedingly. "I didn't know what was on. It was only the radio talk about someone trying to kill that guy Douglas that clued me in. This is the first chance I've had to call. He left half an hour ago. I told the others I was slipping out for some smokes."

"Where are you?" asked the officer urgently. Dalton kept on talking, making his voice shriller.

"Listen, he's got some sort of pass. I saw it when he took his jacket off. It's some sort of White House pass."

"Where are you?" demanded the officer, almost shouting now.

"I'm in a pay phone on We—"

Dalton deepened his voice, partly covered the mouthpiece, and held it away from him.

"Bastard," he hissed in a tone completely different from the shrill voice he had been using. He let the phone drop but made sure it banged against the metal of the booth as it fell. Anyone watching would think he had just dropped it. At the same time he pressed the cradle and cut off the call.

"Hello, hello," the officer shouted in vain.

Dalton replaced the phone in the cradle and walked briskly away.

Ten minutes later he arrived at a tour bus pickup point near the Washington Monument. He caught a glimpse of himself in the reflected glass of the stand: a fresh-faced young man, traveling light and visiting the capital's tourist spots. He rested the travel bag on the ground and waited.

The bus was nearly full when it arrived. It consisted of three interconnected coaches. Some of the tourists got off at his stop, and Dalton squeezed into the second coach.

The passengers were chatting away excitedly. The pretty black tour guide looked smartly efficient in her tight-fitting uniform as she explained their itinerary. All day long, the tour buses shuttled around the city, ferrying visitors to the various places of interest.

Dalton knew the exact route they would follow.

Fifteen minutes later he arrived at the killing ground.

The official reception was on the South Lawn. As Roeder drove around by the front of the White House he saw the demonstration. The police had known well in advance that a large demonstration was being organized and had taken appropriate precautionary measures.

Chartered coaches had brought groups of demonstrators in from the cities with large Irish communities. The green and gold banners of the various Irish-American organizations were unfurled in the sun. Smaller demonstrations had been going on for some weeks prior to the Prime Minister's arrival, but the one today was to be the most effective in terms of number and publicity.

Other smaller banners carried pictures of men with various injuries, which the banners proclaimed had been received while being held in detention in Ireland.

Stewards dressed in easily identifiable red blazers and ties seemed to be plentiful. As the people stepped down from the coaches they were shepherded into the main body of demonstrators. TV crews were standing around smoking and occasionally interviewing people.

Roeder ordered his driver to stop the car. He looked closely at the crowd. Was it possible that the killer was in there amongst them? He felt the sweat in his armpits. The whole area around the White House was saturated with police. Helicopters constantly patrolled overhead. It was inconceivable to think that the man would try here.

The faces in the demonstrating crowd were checked. Those who looked in the slightest way suspicious were taken away for closer questioning. This naturally led to protests from the other demonstrators, but as they were also aware of the assassination fears the protests were perhaps not as strong as they might have been. It did, however, make the situation even more tense.

Roeder's car had hardly stopped when a police officer came up and asked his driver to move on. Roeder identified himself, and after carefully checking his card, the officer still asked him to move on. Roeder nodded approvingly. The men had been ordered to be especially careful in checking identification.

He went to the east gate. There, his credentials were checked and double-checked, his special White House pass notwithstanding. He was kept outside for nearly four minutes before being admitted.

Once inside, he quickly found the man responsible for White House security. He was reassured that everything looked fine. Most of the guests had already arrived. A body-check had been carried out on everybody, regardless of rank.

The guests were mingling on the lawn, sherry glasses in hand. A large tent had been temporarily erected to cater to them.

Roeder walked around looking for anything unusual. He had begun to feel a little more optimistic. How could anyone hope to get through the security? Maybe he was overestimating the killer. Maybe the guy really had just given up.

His two-way radio buzzed.

As he listened to the tape of Dalton's call, which had just come through, Roeder felt the sweat break out on his forehead. He was honest enough to admit that it wasn't just the heat.

He forced himself to think logically. He had no choice but to take the phone call at face value. Apparently, whoever was sheltering the killer wanted out. The phone call was in the Washington area from a pay phone, but they couldn't pin it any closer.

Who had stopped the caller? The killer himself? No, the guy had said he'd left half an hour ago. Probably the caller had been followed by one of his accomplices. Maybe he'd made them suspicious.

Jesus, a White House pass?

He quickly advised the coordinator of White House security of the development, and another identification check was urgently initiated.

Thirty minutes later all of the guests had arrived. No latecomers would be allowed in, no matter how important they were.

Five minutes before the arrival of the Prime Minister, the President appeared. He walked to the pad where the Prime Minister's helicopter would set down.

The demonstrators had begun to chant outside. Their chanting was quite distinct despite the helicopters overhead. Obviously they were well-coached. Their stewards had small loudspeakers and directed the protest.

The Prime Minister's helicopter arrived. Charles Douglas stepped down and was greeted by the President. He was introduced to the First Lady and various dignitaries before both men made their way to a large wooden podium.

The chanting from outside heightened the air of tension inside.

The President's speech was long and wide-ranging. He included a section dealing with the situation in Ireland and pledged the good will and support of his administration toward a peaceful resolution of the problem.

The Prime Minister's speech was short and formal. It also included a section on Ireland in which he thanked the President for his interest and reassured him that the problem was being tackled with the utmost dedication and vigor.

Roeder was anxiously scanning the assembled guests. Suddenly, he saw a young man stand up in the front row. The man had his hand inside his jacket pocket. He was up on his chair before anybody could move.

The shout was still in Roeder's throat as the hand came into view. It was clutching a sheet of paper! The sheet was similar to those that the demonstrators had stuck on the placards outside, showing the allegedly abused detainees.

"Explain this away, Douglas," the young man shouted. You're—"

His protest was abruptly terminated by the four security men who converged on him and hauled him down. He was quickly dragged away from the scene.

The Prime Minister continued as if nothing had happened.

At the end of his speech, the assembled guests applauded politely.

The President and the Prime Minister left the podium and entered the White House building.

Later, it transpired that the lone demonstrator was the son of a well-known politician. He was a bona fide guest. At least security had not been breached.

After a period inside the White House the Prime Minister set off for the Capitol. The demonstrators followed, marching up Pennsylvania Avenue to continue their chanting at the steps of the Capitol.

Roeder went over the phone call in his mind. The only other time the Prime Minister would be at the White House was for the state dinner that evening. Was it possible?

He hurried back to his action center.

• TWENTY-THREE •

ARLINGTON CEMETERY. The burial ground for American military dead since the time of the Civil War.

As Dalton crossed the Arlington Memorial Bridge, which connected the Yankee North with the Old South, he could see the huge cemetery in the distance.

Once over the river, he was on Memorial Drive, a wide, straight avenue that led directly to the entrance to the cemetery. The tour bus passed through the large gates, and drove up to a special parking area. In the parking area the passengers were asked to leave the bus. Those who already had tickets for the tour of the cemetery took their places in the line for another bus that would bring them around the various memorials. Those without tickets went to buy them.

Shortly afterward they were in the new bus and commenced the tour.

As they drove along they looked at the white gravestones stretching away into the distance. The huge cemetery was set on a number of steep hills. Leafy trees cast their long shadows over the rolling acres.

The tour guide pointed out the various sections where the dead of the different wars were laid.

Time did not matter here.

Union and Confederate soldier, World War One infantryman, and Korean pilot were all united in their final resting place. The only slight discrepancy was in the shape of the Union and Confederate gravestones—one round-topped and the other square. Still not quite together. . . .

Occasionally the bus halted, and the tour guide would point out the tombstone of some illustrious soldier. The most recent additions to the cemetery brought tears to the eyes of a few people on the bus. The memories of Vietnam were still vivid.

Dalton checked his watch. No hurry. He would wait until he had a perfect opportunity.

The bus pulled up a steep hill and stopped beside a large colonial house. This was the former home of Confederate leader Robert E. Lee. As soon as the passengers had disembarked to examine the house, the bus moved away. They would be picked up shortly by the next bus that came along.

Dalton walked around the house with the other people. The presence of such a fine house in the unlikely setting of a cemetery was explained by the origins of the cemetery. After the American Civil War, the victorious federal government had decided to select an area which could be used thereafter as a burial site for those who gave their lives in the service of their country.

Feelings were still bitter after the years of conflict. The federal government decided to pick the home of the Confederacy's greatest figure as the site for this new cemetery. No doubt, the irony of Union soldiers being buried in Robert E. Lee's beautiful estate appealed to them.

After walking around the house and gardens for twenty minutes, Dalton boarded another tour bus and set off again.

The next stop was at the Amphitheater, in front of which lay the Tomb of the Unknown Soldier. A single guard from the nearby army base at Fort Myer paced up and down. Despite the intense heat, he was in full parade uniform: white gloves, peaked hat, and thick boots shined to perfection.

Dalton walked into the Amphitheater. Inside was a medal museum showing the various military decorations awarded by different countries. Success or failure, there'd be no medals for him.

Upon reboarding the bus, the tourists had lost a little of the solemnity that the cemetery had imposed on them. The bus brought them to the next setdown point, the gravesites of John and Robert Kennedy.

The Kennedy plot was set in a completely separate section of the cemetery. It lay at the center of a hill, with a semicircular path bringing the visitors up one side of the hill to the gravesites. Here they paused for a few moments before continuing along the path as it curved back down again. A grassy slope stretched up from the gravesides to a white multi-pillared building at the top of the hill.

At the gravesides the visitors maintained a reverent silence. A rectangular stone plot marked the final resting place of the former President. In another plot some yards to the left lay Robert Kennedy, his grave marked by a simple wooden cross. Someone had tossed a single red rose beside the cross.

As the people filed down the hill to the bus, they were strangely silent. So many years had passed since the dreams that died in Dallas.

The bus returned to the ticket office from where the tour of the cemetery had commenced. The people disembarked and boarded another bus that would take them back into Washington. Large numbers of new visitors were lining up to begin the next tour. Theirs would be the final trip of the day.

Dalton joined the new line. He had been satisfied with the first trip round. Security would be no problem.

He boarded the bus and started on his second tour. He had chosen three possible places of quick concealment; the only other vital thing was that none of the tourists spotted him when he made his move.

He took his chance at the first place.

As the people were walking around Robert E. Lee's home and garden, Dalton slipped back to the bus pickup point before the next one had arrived. He casually walked around a bend in the road until he was well-screened from the house. After a careful scan, he quickly slipped in behind a tree. Some dense bushes lay just beyond it, and a few seconds later he was in them and completely concealed from the road.

Shortly afterward he heard the voices of the tourists returning to the bus.

At five o'clock the last tourist bus had left the cemetery, and the large gates were closed.

Dalton lay down amongst the dead.

• TWENTY-FOUR •

HE LAY UNDISTURBED. The silence was occasionally broken by a voice in the distance or a truck going by. The huge cemetery needed a small army of attendants.

Every thirty minutes he stretched his arms and legs to ward off muscular fatigue. It was difficult in the small space and still he suffered the occasional cramp. The sweat poured off his body as the sun beat down. He purposely avoided checking the time since darkness would tell him when he had to move. So he lay on his side and tried not to think.

Slowly the evening crawled toward darkness and the prospect of relief.

When the darkness came it was, as usual, unannounced by twilight. Suddenly the sun had gone and the night was all around. He allowed plenty of time for his eyes to adjust. Shapes that seconds before were just formless lumps now identified themselves as trees.

Luckily there was enough moonlight to give reasonable visibility. He didn't want to use a flashlight if possible. The darkness intensified when the occasional cloud drifted across the face of the moon.

When the night was truly down and his eyes had adjusted, he decided to move. The luminous dial of his watch showed nine-fifty P.M.

The geography of the cemetery was etched in his mind. He made his way amongst the gravestones, using the cover provided by the trees and bushes. He moved very carefully. His destination was quite near, but it took him almost an hour to reach it. Finally, he stood under the branches of a thick, leafy tree.

On his previous visits to the cemetery three months earlier, he had chosen the site where he would assassinate Charles Douglas with painstaking thoroughness. It had to fulfill each of the criteria he had set: access, visibility, and a degree of concealment which would put him in a position to make the hit. The fourth factor, ease of withdrawal, would determine if he lived afterward.

The following day was the sixth of June, the anniversary of the D-Day landings at Normandy. In the morning Prime Minister Charles Douglas would lay a wreath at the Tomb of the Unknown Soldier. Following that, he would lay wreaths at the gravesides of John and Robert Kennedy. This latter ceremony would be at approximately noon.

It was then that Dalton planned to assassinate him.

The tree was thirty yards in from the road, and approximately a hundred and forty yards to the left of the Kennedy plot. The plot was not visible from ground level at this point.

Dalton laid the travel bag on the ground, opened it, and carefully removed the plastic explosive. It was relatively stable until primed with a detonator. The tiny detonators were in a steel box, each one shrouded in thick cotton. A detonator carelessly handled could mutilate a man's hand. He laid the box down beside the explosive on a small sheet of polyethylene.

He then removed the special transmitter and receivers he had bought on his first day in New York. Unscrewing the covering plates from the three receivers, he bared two wires in each of them and laid them down on the polyethylene. Each receiver was about the same size as a cigarette pack.

Next he turned his attention to the actual transmitter. This had a simple on-off switch on one side and three separate buttons on the other, connecting the transmitter to whichever receiver the operator wished to contact. He removed the plate from the back of the transmitter and pried the three buttons from the side. This allowed him to pull the wires through the open back. From the travel bag he obtained a plastic timer, which had three watch-size dials set on the front and numbered in sequence. At the back of each dial was a small metal stud. He attached the correct wires from the transmitter to each stud and then set the dials at the timing he required. Finally, he taped the timer to the transmitter and returned it to the travel bag, which he concealed in some bushes near the tree.

Gathering up the receivers and explosive in the polyethylene sheet, he moved away from the tree up the hill. He was moving in the direction of the white-pillared building above the Kennedy plot. Here two soldiers maintained a lonely vigil over the graves below. They had an unimpeded view straight down the hill to the plot.

Dalton skirted silently around the back of the building. He could hear the rasp of the sentries' boots as they paced the regulation number of steps in each direction. Far from being unwanted, this lonely graveside vigil was regarded as a great honor.

His destination was about thirty yards beyond the white building. At this point the ground dipped sharply and the foliage beyond gave adequate cover.

Once there, he knelt down and gently laid the polyethylene on the ground. He removed the plastic explosive and divided it into three sections, each weighing about half a pound. Taking an atomizer from his pocket, he quickly sprayed its contents over the explosive.

Next he took one of the receivers and attached a detonator to the exposed wires at the back. The other end of the detonator he gingerly stuck into a section of the plastic explosive. Finally, he molded the explosive around the receiver.

He repeated the exercise with the other two receivers. When he was finished he had three radio-controlled bombs, relatively harmless until signaled.

It took him over twenty minutes to conceal the bombs, each within ten feet of each other and a hundred and thirty yards uphill of where the wreath-laying ceremony would be held.

Satisfied with their concealment, he commenced his return journey. He skirted behind the white-pillared building, and gradually the sentries' footsteps faded until once again he stood at the base of the tree.

His watch showed one thirty-five A.M.

Retrieving the travel bag from the bushes, he removed some clothes from it and laid them out neatly on the grass. He quickly peeled off his sweat-soaked shirt and jeans and dressed in the new clothes, then took a thin plastic-coated rope from the bag. It was weighted slightly at each end and despite its delicate appearance was reinforced with a strong core of tensile steel.

He stood under the tree and breathed deeply for a few seconds. The first branch was well above head level. He was just about to toss one end of the rope over this branch when he heard the sound.

He grabbed the travel bag and slid in behind the bushes. Seconds later, the glow of headlights appeared in the distance. As the lights drew nearer, he slipped the .38 out of the travel bag.

Without slowing down the jeep passed by. The shadowy outlines of four figures were visible as it continued along the winding road up the hill toward the white building.

The motor cut out, and then silence. He closed his eyes and strained to hear. One voice speaking sharply. Then, silence again.

Three minutes later he heard the motor start up once more. As the jeep came nearer, its lights pierced the darkness around him. Again the brief silhouette of four people.

Dalton relaxed. Of course. Driver, duty officer, and the two guards, their sentry duty finished and their reliefs in position.

When the sound of the jeep had died away he returned to the tree. Seconds later he had the rope over the branch and both ends grasped in his hands. He knotted one end around the grip of the travel bag and, using the leverage of his feet against the bark, quickly hauled himself up onto the branch. He then hauled the travel bag up after him. With the rope tied securely around his midriff, he continued climbing until the white building finally came into view. He breathed a sigh of relief. Not much farther. A little higher up and he would have a perfect view of the gravesite.

Eventually, he settled for the angle formed by two thick branches with the trunk of the tree. This allowed him to support his back, with his legs straddling one of the branches. The leaves were thick enough here to give adequate cover but not so thick that they would obstruct his view of the plot.

The climb up had temporarily exhausted him, but he couldn't afford to rest just yet. Wearily, he continued.

Removing the radio transmitter from the travel bag he taped it to a small branch. It would need to be repositioned when dawn came. He retrieved some of the sandwiches and Coke that he had stored in the travel bag and then secured the bag to a branch with two leather straps. Finally, he strapped himself to one of the branches and leaned back exhausted.

He checked his watch. Two-thirty A.M.

Now for the long wait. . . .

* * *

Forty minutes later, he almost fell asleep. Too dangerous. The straps securing him to the tree would stop him from tilting over, but they wouldn't be strong enough to hold the full weight of his body. He had to keep awake. He opened a small box and swallowed three concentrated dextrose lozenges. As his blood sugar rose, it gave him a quick burst of energy. He had decided long ago never to use any form of drug to ward off sleep. Although these achieved their purpose, they also interfered with normal reactions, made things seem easier than they were—just as dangerous as falling asleep. He would rely on the high sugar content of the Coke and the lozenges to keep him alert.

He turned his head to the side. In the distance he could see the white tombstones reflected in the moonlight. Although he had lived with death for so long, the prospect of spending such a long night in the vast cemetery was not a pleasant one. In the darkness his mind sought to occupy itself. At least he partly determined his own destiny. How many of the soldiers buried there had ever had that chance? Just so much cannon fodder for the generals and politicians as they pushed their little, colored pins around on maps.

He remembered the contempt his grandfather had expressed for these armchair generals. Some weeks before his death, they had gone on their last fishing trip together. They had gone to a small lake in Wicklow. It was a beautiful spring evening, and as they waited for the fish to bite Kevin's question had taken his grandfather completely by surprise.

"Why did you change your mind about fighting in the troubles, Grandad?" he asked.

His grandfather looked at him sharply and then out over the lake. "It's a long story, Kevin."

"I'd really like to know," the boy persisted.

His grandfather looked at him and smiled. "You're just like me, never take no for an answer."

He looked back over the lake. "Well, since you're so interested I'll tell you." He paused before continuing. "You know I was a soldier in the British Army once, don't you? A damn good soldier too. They gave me a lot of medals to show just how good I was."

The boy missed the mocking tone.

"Each of those medals represented a battle where a lot of people died."

"Daddy told me about them," interrupted Kevin. "He told me about one where twenty thousand people died in one day."

"That's right lad. On the Somme. That terrible first day. I was a sergeant then." His grandfather's voice was sad. "Thousands of young men. Some of them were really just boys, a few years older than yourself. A lot of them were Irish too, but at least then it didn't matter where we came from. It really didn't matter. We all just wanted to live."

His grandfather seemed to be far away now.

"Do you know an Englishman saved my life that day?" he said abruptly.

"A Black and Tan?" asked Kevin incredulously.

"Not that scum. They weren't real soldiers," replied his grandfather with contempt.

"No, this fellow was a Tynesider. They went over just after us. I'll tell you this, Kevin, I've never been so scared in my life. Never before or since."

"What happened?" the boy asked, his attention riveted on his grandfather.

"We ran and ran. We were told that we wouldn't meet with much resistance, that our big guns had flattened the Germans. What they didn't tell us was that the Germans were just too smart for us. They knew when we'd be coming. They just dug deeper trenches and waited till we had finished pounding the earth above them. For days we bombarded their trenches. When our guns finally stopped, it was their signal that we were coming. They had dug in so deep that they needed lifts to get back up to the surface.

"To get to them we had to go over open ground with barbed wire all across it. We'd been told that our bombardment had destroyed it. That we'd just have to stroll through."

His grandfather shook his head bitterly. "They lied to us, Kevin. Those generals in their safe little command posts well behind the lines knew what was coming. But they had decided to use us as a battering ram. It was clear that we'd be decimated once we were out in the open."

He explained to Kevin's puzzled face. "Decimated, Kevin—that just means slaughtered. Some of our fellows actually reached the German trenches but most of them were cut down in the open ground. I'll never forget the endless clatter of the machine guns. I got to within a hundred yards when we heard the signal to retreat. They relayed it on big loudspeakers so we could hear it. I turned and started running back. In my hurry I ran bang into a big coil of barbed wire. That wire was terrible, Kevin, it just pulled you in! I had to throw down my rifle to try and tear myself clear. Our lads were running back as fast as they could. The Tynesiders had come up on our left and they were turning to get back too.

"The Germans had come out of their trenches and were charging toward us. I couldn't get out, Kevin. I pulled and pulled and ripped my hands on that damn wire. I was nearly free when a German reached me. Do you know what he had in his hands? A bloody big shovel. That's what was often used out there instead of a bayonet. A fine-honed shovel was more effective and didn't break or stick once it had been used. It was just like a sword."

Kevin's mouth was dry. "What happened, Grandad?" he whispered.

"I pulled as desperately as I could, but I knew I wouldn't make it. The German was just about to take my head off with that shovel when one of the Tynesiders dived at him from my left side and bayoneted him. God must have meant to spare me because somehow I tore free at that moment. I turned and ran like hell."

"What happened to the English soldier?"

His grandfather shook his head. "I just don't know. Whether or not he survived that day I'll never know. All I saw was him turning and running back toward our lines. I went around to their trenches that night to try and find him but it was impossible."

He paused for a moment.

"He didn't have to do it, Kevin. While most of our fellows were running back with the devil at their heels that Tynesider deliberately ran toward the Germans. He must have seen me nearly clear of the wire and made the conscious decision to risk his own life. Out there, in that hell, it was a tremendous thing to do."

"So that's why you didn't want to fight the English afterward," said Kevin.

"I suppose that was partly the reason. You know, he's no different from us, the ordinary Englishman. He was as much sinned against in his own country as we were here. He woke up after that war, though. Never again would the young men go like sheep to their slaughter like in my time. Another kind of conflict started in England when the troops came home, though no guns were used. The people began to shake off the blood-suckers and the parasites that had feasted themselves on their misery for so long."

His grandfather's voice had taken on a hard edge.

"Do you know, Kevin, that after that battle almost every one of our officers under the rank of captain had been killed. Almost every one! The battalion was just a skeleton. Two months later they made me an officer. My eyes were well-opened by then, I can tell you. I was an officer all right, and I'd been commissioned in the hardest way possible. I mixed with the English officers on a different basis once I'd been commissioned. There was a world of difference between being an officer and an enlisted man. Obviously, the fact that I hadn't actually been a cadet at Sandhurst couldn't be overlooked. Even out in the mud with the rats and the endless suffering, the social distinctions were rigidly observed. But I was still an officer and therefore accepted in an offhand sort of way.

"Now, Kevin, you needn't think that this made me resentful of them. Not at all. In fact, I didn't give a damn, and they knew it. They hated me for that. They were conditioned to think that their silly niceties meant something, but I only told them how foolish they were. They knew I was a socialist.

"To be fair, some of the younger ones weren't too bad. The higher up they went the more rigid they became. As they fell out of contact with the poor, ordinary soldiers doing the fighting they became completely callous. The younger ones, the lieutenants and captains, at least shared the danger with the men. Even still, toward the end of the war, a lot of those officers were shot in battle by their own men. Some good ones as well as bad. They had to watch their backs damn carefully."

"Why did they make you an officer if they didn't like you?" asked Kevin.

"Well, it certainly wasn't for the love of me," his grandfather smiled. "No, the practicalities of the situation left them with very little choice. There weren't many left who had survived two full years in the trenches. I wouldn't have taken the commission either except that I thought I might be in a better position to help the men. Anyway, I survived another two years after that. When I came home to Ireland I can tell you I'd seen enough bloodshed to last a lifetime. I never wanted to hear or see a gun again. I became a pacifist."

"Yes, Daddy told me that," said Kevin.

"We had some of them in the army during the war. They used to drive the ambulances. Just as dangerous as being a soldier. At the beginning they got terrible abuse. More from the people who were safe at home than from the lads in the trenches. Toward the end, the soldiers looked on them as having a great deal more sense than the rest of the country. A lot of eyes had been opened over the years. At least those that hadn't been closed forever.

"So you see, Kevin, I'd had my fill of killing. Back in Ireland again, I thought that it wouldn't be long before we achieved self-determination here. At the same time, and just as important, we'd get rid of the blood-suckers in this country as well as in England. We had a lot of friends amongst the people over there, you know."

His grandfather sighed. "I suppose my experiences during the war clouded my judgment. I thought that we would just have to be patient. With the arrival of the Black and Tans, I knew that patience wasn't enough. I saw then that we'd have to take the first step ourselves. The people in power had too strong a grip on us. The time for ordinary people to exert their influence would never come if we didn't loosen that grip. Those friends that I mentioned in England helped us as much as possible. They tried to educate the public that the repression of ordinary people in Ireland was no longer acceptable. In the end, of course, we won through, but it left us with a bitter legacy."

His grandfather noticed the sun slowly declining at the back of the lake. He stood up and tousled Kevin's hair. "Anyway, Kevin, thank God you'll never have to worry about these things. . . . "

Irritably, Dalton chased his wandering thoughts away. The luxury of moralizing was something he had lost a long time ago. This was not the time or the place to indulge in idle speculation. If he failed, death would solve his questions forever. He did not intend to die.

He checked the time again. Four twenty-five A.M.

He looked over at the Kennedy plot. They would, of course, be horrified at Douglas' assassination in such a reverent place. To many it would seem like a desecration. But more, much more than that, they would be stunned into awareness. In death Kennedy had drawn a thousand times more scrutiny than in life. At least his image had remained relatively untarnished. But Douglas and his government had too many skeletons buried in Ireland. They would be pinned on the microscope and torn apart. The nettle of mindless partition would be firmly grasped and pulled up by its roots.

The darkness was beginning to thin a little. Dawn was about to break.

He must not fail now.

• TWENTY-FIVE •

A WAITER, immaculately dressed in jet-black trousers and a starched white jacket, approached the Prime Minister. Roeder had positioned himself so that he could see the main table of the dining room. He was also dressed in a waiter's uniform. It bothered him that he couldn't see the waiter's face. No matter how he moved his head, the man's face still remained in shadow.

Something was wrong. He knew it. He started to run toward the waiter. As he drew nearer he saw the gun that had suddenly appeared in the man's hand. The guests' faces looked up in alarm.

Oh, God, why was he moving so slowly!

The Prime Minister had still not looked up. The waiter was just beside him as Roeder threw himself at him. Now the guests were screaming in horror. Desperately he swung the man around. The gun fired simultaneously. Slowly the waiter turned until he was facing Roeder. The agent recoiled in horror. The man's face was that of the injured detainee that he had seen on the poster that afternoon!

He felt the hands of the guests on him. Pulling urgently. He tried to brush them off but they kept pulling.

He woke up in his temporary bed, saturated in sweat. The young agent who had woken him looked at him curiously.

"It's okay, okay. Bad dream," Roeder muttered. He rubbed his eyes and forced himself to appear wide awake.

Still dark outside.

Christ, this one had really got to him. He had attended the White House dinner in the waiter's uniform as in his dream. Every single guest had had a new pass issued and been thoroughly rescreened. A new catering staff was provided for the state dinner. The guards responsible for White House security had been replaced by a completely new team. Unless the killer could make himself invisible, there was no way in.

Still he had worried. The whole damn night he had worried. It was only when the last guest had left and the Prime Minister had retired for the night that he had relaxed.

When it was over he had returned exhausted to the FBI headquarters.

Surely the odds were completely against the killer now. All that remained for him was to run. The young agent broke into his thoughts.

"Sir, we've identified him!"

Roeder jerked to attention.

"British Intelligence has made him. His name is Kevin Dalton and they reckon he's taken out at least twelve of their men."

"Jesus, twelve killings," Roeder whistled.

"Yes, sir, and from their assessment he's a completely ruthless operator. Their information is that he won't be deflected by anything. We've just got to nail him. . . ."

British Intelligence in Ireland had been trying to identify Maitland-Jones' killer since the time of the murder. He had been highly regarded after his long years in Intelligence, and many of their present operatives in Ireland had been personally trained by him.

In the few days after the killing, numerous people with Republican sympathies were arrested. The roundup and the questioning that followed produced some worthwhile results. Unfortunately, despite the arrest of some wanted men and the discovery of large amounts of arms and explosive caches, the knowledge gained did not help them to solve their main problem.

The people arrested were shown the composite sketch of the bearded suspect wired across from America. Nobody could or would identify the man.

The longer their efforts remained unrewarded, the more intense the political pressure became on the security forces. The government was extremely disturbed by the regular FBI reports. If only they could put some substance to the shadow, something the Americans could work on. . . .

The solution was indirectly given to them by an old lady in Belfast.

One of the men arrested on the second day of the roundups was a so-called "officer" in the enemy organization. He was one of the few men who knew of Kevin Dalton's existence. He had not met Dalton for some years and was not aware of the full extent of his involvement in the Organization. Once before, at the start of the troubles, he had been interned for a year but was not wanted for any specific crime at present. He had been living openly in Belfast since his release from internment. The Leader had called him out of Belfast one week before the Army Council meeting in Dublin. The man had not been given a reason but was kept well-occupied in Dublin as soon as he arrived. Although curious at his sudden move, he accepted it without question.

When an inconsequential phone call to a relative in Derry revealed that his mother was close to death after a heart attack, the man reacted without thinking. He crossed back over the border into the North, using an unapproved road. Ten minutes later he was stopped at a random-check army roadblock and his name radioed in for routine processing through the army central computer. When it identified him as a known Republican, and a former internee, he was promptly arrested and brought to Belfast for questioning.

When shown the American composite of Dalton his reaction was closely observed. His mind was on his sick mother and he made a slip. To the interrogators who had shown the sketch to many other sympathizers his reaction was suspicious enough to warrant further interrogation. This resulted in a grudging admission that he might have seen the man somewhere before.

When the FBI received Dalton's bogus telephone call in Washington, British Intelligence was still no nearer identifying the suspect than when they had started the roundup. The only person who admitted to ever having seen him before was this man they were questioning in Belfast. They were sure that he could give them a name, and as their frustration grew, they concentrated their efforts on him.

The man had now realized how badly they wanted an identification. At first, he resisted all efforts to make him cooperate further.

It took several more hours before he eagerly identified the man in the picture as Kevin Dalton. He also told them what he knew about the killings that had puzzled them for so long. He wasn't sure how many of them were down to Dalton, but he didn't know of anyone else operating in such a way. He would gladly have told them anything that they wanted to know.

The combination of sedatives and hallucinogenic drugs they used had been carefully monitored. First, the reduction of his anxiety and the lessening of interest in his immediate surroundings; then, the induction of vivid delusions of grandeur; finally, the increase in his receptability to carefully phrased suggestions. The two anesthetists and the psychiatrist worked together to determine the various dosages with the utmost precision. The only slight problem was the not unexpected laryngeal spasm after two hours, which was easily countered by the rapid administration of emergency oxygen.

He couldn't wait to tell them all about the great plans they had for the future and the men who would achieve that future. He knew that it was happening, but he didn't care. His own mind held out for as long as possible but in the end it really didn't matter anymore. . . .

"Anything?" Roeder asked the senior agent who had been monitoring the action center while he slept.

"Nothing, sir. We haven't any lead on that phone call and nobody's reported seeing any sort of struggle at a phone booth. No missing person reports either."

Christ. Another day of it! He was damn weary.

Once again he went over the Prime Minister's schedule for the day.

No public appearance until eleven forty-five that morning. Then the D-Day services at Arlington. Smithsonian tour starting at three. Live television interview at six. Private meetings with various Senators for the rest of the evening. Fly to Houston next morning.

He checked the security arrangements for each part of the day. He would at least try to have the Prime Minister persuaded to cancel the Smithsonian tour, though almost certainly he would be wasting his time. Charles Douglas had been explicit. No alterations to the proposed schedule. Nothing that could be taken as a concession to terrorist pressure.

It was as if just ignoring the killer would make him go away. Roeder decided that he would continue checking the Prime Minister's security personally.

Through the venetian blinds he saw the first streaks of dawn.

· TWENTY-SIX ·

DALTON WAS wide awake now. The new dawn had dispersed his somber mood. From now on he would act with total certainty.

He unstrapped himself from the branch and checked the security of the travel bag and transmitter. Taking the Armalite from the travel bag, he fitted the telescopic sights and hooked the shoulder strap over his right shoulder. He glanced in the direction of the target area and started to move out along a thick branch.

He selected a position where he could lay almost flat out on the branch, and, by leaning slightly to the left, was well supported by a second branch. Through a gap in the leaves he had an uninterrupted view of the target area.

He adjusted the sights slightly. He was a little farther away than he had estimated, but still well within range. He sighted a few times on the front of the graveside.

From that range he was totally confident.

He edged back to the transmitter, and untaped it from its branch. Returning to his firing position, he retaped it level with where his left hand would be supporting the gun. Everything had to be smooth and automatic.

The timer which he had connected to the transmitter was like a clock, with an overall scale of zero to sixty seconds. He now set it for ten seconds. This meant that when he pressed the release button he would have ten seconds in which to sight and shoot. When the timer reached zero, the first radio bomb would explode. The second bomb would explode one second later, followed by the third at the same interval. Three separate explosions within two seconds. By slightly staggering the explosions, he would create a screen of noise for those two seconds. The clay would be blown up over a space of thirty feet on the other side of the plot, well away from him.

The first explosion would be his signal to fire. The noise screen should allow him time to fire two shots. At least, the bomb diversion would completely hide the source of the rifle shots. At most, it would confuse the security personnel and buy him precious time.

He returned to the travel bag, removed the radio and earphones, and strapped himself into the same position as before. He checked the early bulletins. They led with the story of the White House demonstration and the massive security at the Senate. There was an urgent appeal from the police for anyone who had seen a man attacked yesterday afternoon at a public pay phone to contact them immediately.

The D-Day services and the Prime Minister's proposed attendance at Arlington also received a brief mention. Dalton was relieved. The one nagging doubt he had had was that they might back off. Now that it was publicly confirmed, there was no way the Prime Minister could pull out. Not Charles Douglas.

Switching off the radio he returned it to the travel bag, having all the information he needed.

He missed the urgent bulletin five minutes later identifying him as the wanted man.

The buses bringing the first visitors of the day to the cemetery were due to arrive at nine A.M. Many people would also come by car on the anniversary of D-Day. No private cars would be allowed inside the cemetery. Special buses would collect the people at the main gate and ferry them around inside. This would be the only gate open that morning. American ex-servicemen and ordinary civilians would not take kindly to the fact that every single one of them would be subjected to a thorough search.

Dalton had only just replaced the radio in the travel bag when he became aware of the faraway whine of the helicopters. As they became more audible he heard a new sound, that of approaching motor vehicles. He listened carefully. From the chug of their engines they sounded like trucks. His guess was confirmed a few minutes later when three heavy military trucks pulled in along the road well down to his right.

How many men would they use? It was impossible for them to thoroughly search the whole cemetery, so logically they would concentrate on the places where the Prime Minister would be most exposed, in particular, where the wreath-laying ceremonies would occur.

He listened for the sound of barking but couldn't hear any. Good, no dogs. He had wondered if they would actually use dogs in the cemetery. It was possible before the gates had been opened to the public, but unlikely afterward. Even if they gave a tracker some of the clothes he had worn in New York, there were so many scents in the cemetery that it would be almost impossible for the dog. Just in case, he had always worn a strong deodorant. The colorless liquid that he had sprayed on the explosive during the night would mask the smell it emitted. This smell, though undetectable to humans, was quite distinctive to a dog trained in sniffing out explosives. The spray was not completely effective, but unless a dog was brought directly over the bombs, it should be sufficient. Although these dogs were highly effective in confined spaces, out in the open there were too many distracting smells.

The searchers systematically set about their task. The nature and size of the area meant that they had to be fairly superficial. Unless they were exceedingly lucky they would never find the small cigarette-sized bombs hidden in the shrubbery well up from the Kennedy plot.

He could see some of them in the clearing around the plot. They started there and spread outward. Every now and then he heard twigs snapping as one of them passed directly under his tree.

The search was completed at eight-thirty A.M. Afterward, the security men were strategically deployed in the foliage around the plot.

The first visitors entered the cemetery at exactly nine A.M., arriving in continuous streams after that. The area seventy yards around the plot had been cordoned off. To compensate for this the visitors were allowed to go onto the open space above the gravesides, the nearest ones still being seventy yards away. The agents mingled watchfully amongst them.

As the morning passed, the continuous bus loads of people made their presence felt. Snatches of conversation occasionally drifted up to Dalton, mainly American but some foreign accents as well.

He checked the time. Eleven-ten.

Charles Douglas had risen early that morning. Despite the little fracas at the White House reception yesterday, he was well pleased with the tour to date. He knew he had made a good impression where it mattered. Indeed, even the media were now presenting him in a more favorable light than before. In many ways this talk about an assassin had proved useful, generating a surprisingly large amount of sympathy for him as the intended victim. Still it was a bit irritating. . . .

An aide informed him that it was time to leave for Arlington. Douglas subjected himself to a critical last-minute check in the full-length mirror before leaving the Embassy and entering the waiting limousine.

The Prime Minister's party arrived at the cemetery at eleven forty-one.

He was driven very quickly to the first wreath-laying ceremony at the Tomb of the Unknown Soldier. His arrival was timed so that he could lay the wreath after the shortest possible interval. No speeches, no frills. He was at the site for a total of only seven minutes before he set off again to repeat the exercise at the Kennedy plot.

Douglas was quite satisfied with this timing. The TV and newspaper pictures of the ceremony would be impressive. He would hammer home his message in the television interview that evening.

His limousine was custom-built, with a reinforced carriage and bullet-proof windows. Dark curtains screened the back seat to outside eyes. A sniper shooting at the moving car would have to be very lucky. Two other limousines, each containing FBI personnel, moved in front and behind the Prime Minister's car, and a motorcycle escort headed the cavalcade.

The limousine moved quickly through the cemetery to the Kennedy plot.

Carl Roeder had been present at the first ceremony. Nervously he had walked around amongst the crowds of people eagerly craning forward to see the proceedings.

Fifteen minutes before he had set off for Arlington, he had received a sketch wired across from British Intelligence. It was based on the description that they had obtained from the man in Belfast. They didn't know how accurate it was as the man hadn't seen Dalton for some years, but in the absence of an actual photograph, it was the best they could do.

Roeder had compared his own composite with the new British one. Some similarities, but quite a few differences as well. From the British Intelligence report it was obvious that the American composite was sufficiently accurate to enable the man they were interrogating to recognize it as Kevin Dalton. He scanned the faces in the crowd, looking for the two possible faces of the killer.

As soon as the Prime Minister laid his wreath, Roeder left the ceremony and hurried ahead so that he could be at the Kennedy plot before Douglas arrived.

The crowd here was not as large as at the main ceremony. Roeder checked with his security coordinator and was reassured that everything seemed normal. All going well, the Prime Minister would be out of the cemetery in less than fifteen minutes.

It would be a relief to have it over with. Security here was a nightmare. Acre upon acre of hilly ground. Restlessly the agent walked amongst the crowd. As he walked his eyes again scanned the faces and his mind turned over the problem.

The guy had a high-velocity rifle. He had a handgun. He had a small amount of explosive. Three possible methods of killing.

They had combed the ground around the plot itself for a concealed bomb. The amount of the explosive would be enough to kill a man, but it would have to explode just beside him. The killer could, of course, strap the explosive to himself, run across to the Prime Minister, and use himself as a human bomb. Naturally he would kill himself as well, but to a fanatic that wouldn't matter. The agents ringed around the area had strict orders. Anyone that broke through the rope barrier was to be immediately restrained and arrested. Anyone resembling the suspect who broke through and approached within a hundred feet of the Prime Minister was to be shot after a warning. The agents were ordered to shoot to disable at this distance unless the person appeared to be armed. In that case he was to be shot dead.

Roeder had begun to respect the man he hunted. The fellow's political views were not of the slightest interest to him. His respect was professional, not personal. A political fanatic maybe, but anyone who could evade them for so long was a very dangerous opponent. The information on Dalton's past activities in Ireland had strongly reinforced this assessment.

But the killer was not invisible. He couldn't expect to get into the cemetery with a gun and avoid being searched. Not this morning.

If that phone call last evening was accurate, and if the man had not run and was still intending to try for a hit, he would have to be working off the cuff. Just hoping for a chance. If the phone call was accurate. . . .

Yesterday, in the heat of the moment, they had had to assume that it was bona fide, and they based their immediate security planning on this. All of their investigations since then hadn't turned up any missing persons or bodies. That had worried him. The killer's actions to date had been cool and planned. If the phone call was not what it seemed, then the conclusion was inescapable. Last night they had tried to match up a voice print with the recording they had of the phone call to Helen Taverne in New York, but the result was inconclusive. He had ordered an extra intensive search of the cemetery at first light, but the sheer size made it so damn difficult.

His thoughts were interrupted by the arrival of two helicopters directly overhead. Their presence heralded the imminent arrival of the Prime Minister's party.

One minute later the black limousine pulled up at the plot.

• TWENTY-SEVEN •

DALTON WAS READY NOW. In the few minutes before the Prime Minister's arrival he had added the final touch to his plan. He had avoided putting on the jacket for as long as possible. It mustn't look too creased. He buttoned it right up to the collar. The black patent shoes were a little scuffed from the climb, so he rubbed them down with a white handkerchief until they shone.

He was dressed in the full ceremonial uniform of the Third Infantry regiment assigned to guard Arlington Cemetery.

He had had the uniform made in Ireland prior to his departure; the navy blue serge of the jacket blended well with the lighter blue of the trousers. A yellow stripe ran down the outside of the trousers, but, unlike the real uniform, this could be detached, as it was only pressed on with adhesive tabs.

The jacket was that of an officer in the regiment, with yellow stripes circling the cuffs. On the right breast were his officer's tabs and on the left he had sewn some campaign medals and ribbons. He had been especially careful that these medals were sewn tight and didn't jingle together. The .38 made a slight bulge under the jacket.

The peaked cap had a matching yellow stripe around the brim and a U.S. Army badge at the front. It was now taped on the branch beside him.

A real member of the regiment would see that the uniform was not quite accurate but would have to look hard to pinpoint the differences.

Dalton heard the increased helicopter noise overhead. They were his biggest worry. How they reacted would be crucial. He looked along the three-quarter-mile stretch of road that he could see from his vantage point in the tree. A tour bus had just come into view. During the morning the buses had been passing by every few minutes. Some of them were stopping at the Kennedy plot, while others continued past on their way to one of the other sites in the cemetery.

He didn't know how long the Prime Minister would be at the graveside. The exact timing of the hit would be determined by the appearance of a tour bus. He would wait until he could see one approaching. When it was about half a mile away he had calculated that he would have one minute to act. After he fired he would shinny down the tree. While coming down, he would be screened from the helicopters by the leafy branches until the very end. It was likely that they would be scanning either the actual scene of the assassination or the point where the bombs had exploded, one hundred and thirty yards up from the plot and well away to the right. He would jump down the final denuded portion of the tree on their blind side. A quick sprint would have him on the road and screened by the thick bushes along the road except from direct overhead surveillance. If any security guard was near the tree and saw him dropping onto the ground he would have to shoot him.

He would have to be down the tree and in position on the road just before the bus came around the bend. But only just before. If he was waiting too long he would be visible to the helicopters.

This was where he needed the luck. The confusion of the explosions and the assassination would be enormous. He had seen enough explosions to know the sort of panic that followed amongst the bystanders. It was to be expected that some of them would start to run wildly from the scene.

If everything went according to plan, and if he was lucky, the helicopters might not pick him out as he boarded the bus. They would see the bus coming along before the hit, but then the explosions and the assassination would rivet them. By the time they came to checking the bus again he could be on it unnoticed. Even if they did see him, the army uniform might throw them.

He had a chance. It was enough.

He concentrated on the kill.

Prime Minister Charles Douglas stepped out of his car. His expression was composed and solemn, in strict keeping with the occasion. Despite his pragmatic and unemotional nature he was moved by the vastness of the cemetery and the reverence it generated. Rememberance Day at home always affected him in the same way. The D-Day ceremony had brought back poignant memories of his own Royal Navy days on the artic convoys.

Although protocol did not strictly require that he lay a wreath at the Kennedy gravesite while in Arlington, he had specifically requested to do so. His own personal view was that Kennedy had been overrated, but the gesture would be well-appreciated.

He stood in reverent silence about ten feet from the graveside.

Dalton watched.

No sign of a bus yet. Supposing none came during the ceremony? The idea of not going ahead with the hit, even if he couldn't get out afterward, was unthinkable. He would just have to take his chances.

He checked the graveside again.

The Prime Minister was standing to attention, flanked by various officials. Dalton could easily distinguish the security men from the officials. Obviously they wanted to make their presence felt. Nicely cut suits and flowers in their lapels, but the constant scanning motion of their heads identified them.

A lone army bugler started to play "The Star-Spangled Banner." The Prime Minister stood rigidly to attention, hand clasped on his chest. The roped-off visitors were completely hushed.

Dalton scanned the road again. Nothing!

He felt the cold sweat on his face. Soon it would be too late.

And then he saw it! Coming around the bend three quarters of a mile away!

He waited calmly until the gap had closed to half a mile.

The bugler had stopped playing. Douglas held the wreath in his hands and moved forward to place it on the grave.

Dalton moved smoothly into his firing position. He pressed the timer button on the transmitter and the pointer started to move.

It took him three seconds to sight on Douglas' head. He aimed at the temple region just in front of the left ear.

The Prime Minister laid the wreath and stepped back. He stood to attention as the bugler started to play again. The music haunted the otherwise silent scene.

Dalton counted the seconds to himself. He reached zero just before the timer pointer.

The first explosion came. After a half-second reaction gap, Dalton squeezed the trigger twice. His second shot followed the first so quickly that it seemed like one shot.

Both high-velocity bullets almost blew Charles Douglas' head off.

• TWENTY-EIGHT •

DALTON WAS MOVING NOW. As the noise of the third explosion died away he hooked the Armalite into a leather loop on the branch and furiously shinnied down the tree.

His luck held. Nobody visible. He dropped onto the ground and pressed the peaked cap onto his head. Three seconds later he was on the road. He could hear the screaming behind him. The bus took another ten seconds to round the bend.

Dalton raised an imperious arm.

The driver had heard the bangs. He was an ex-soldier and he knew what an explosion sounded like. When he saw the army officer urgently signaling him down, he quickly braked.

The officer jumped in beside him.

"Move it," he shouted urgently. "There's a damn battle going on up there. Get these civilians the hell out of here."

The driver reacted unquestioningly to the uniform.

The bus moved along the road. As it passed below the Kennedy plot, Dalton could see the confusion. People were running around wildly, some screaming hysterically.

Better than he expected.

The bus pulled away from the scene.

"What the hell happened back there?" asked the driver.

Dalton ignored him. "Hurry up, I want these civilians out of the firing line. Where's your intercom?"

The driver gave him the intercom and Dalton switched it on.

"Remain calm," he admonished the passengers. "A terrorist assassination squad has attempted to kill the British Prime Minister. As a precaution, I want you all out of the area as quickly as possible. I repeat, remain calmly in your seats."

The passengers buzzed with excitement. Dalton switched the

intercom off and faced to the front again.

Would they close the gates of the cemetery? If they reacted quickly they would. He could only hope that the confusion would delay them. The helicopters looking down would see other tour buses along the route. Nothing to pick his bus out, unless they had sighted him boarding the bus.

If the gates were shut, it was all over for him. He could see the walls of the cemetery approaching ahead. Now he could see the gates.

Open! Two other buses were in front and about to pass through.

Dalton shouted at the driver. "Pull in outside the gates. Get everybody out, they'll want to talk to you."

When he was a hundred yards away, Dalton waved his arms frantically toward the gates. He hopped off the bus as it slowed down and raced up to the security men. The bus continued on through.

"Get those goddamn gates shut," he ordered. "They've tried to kill the Prime Minister. It looks like there's a squad of them in there. Nothing more gets in or out of the cemetery."

Again the uniform and tone of command were enough. The security men were galvanized into action.

Dalton was careful to be on the outside when the gates were locked.

Roeder was numb. He had been amongst the crowd looking down on the ceremony when the first explosion came. Like most of the people, the explosion had jerked his head away from the plot and up the hill. When he had turned back after the third explosion, the Prime Minister's body had already hit the ground.

Roeder raced through the crowds of people toward the scene of the explosion. People were screaming and running in all directions. He pushed them aside, his identification label flapping on his breast.

Some of the other agents had already reached the bomb craters. Roeder shouted at them to move in and start combing the area. A helicopter was circling directly overhead. He contacted it on his radio and quickly identified himself.

"Can you see anything?" he shouted urgently.

"Nothing yet, sir."

"Stay over this area," he ordered. "He must have been in a tree.

Guide the people on the ground."

"Roger."

Roeder jammed the radio into his pocket and raced back down the hill. He pushed his way through the knot of people surrounding the slain Prime Minister. Another helicopter circled overhead. Some of the people were staring in shock at the blood and skull fragments.

The Prime Minister's body was splayed out like a rag doll. The bullets had caused so much destruction that it was impossible to determine exactly where the first impact had occurred. An autopsy would determine that later. It would determine the angle of the shots, the fact that two bullets were fired, and the range at which they were fired.

Roeder could not tear his horrified gaze away. He felt the bitterness of failure and the deep surge of hatred for the man who had beaten him. The nights of strain and the horror of the Prime Minister's shattered body had finally caught up with him.

A woman's hysterical screaming pierced his senses. He turned and slapped her sharply on the face. Her screaming died down to a continuous sobbing.

The act shook Roeder out of his lethargy. Some of the agents were standing around, a mixture of bewilderment and guilt on their faces.

"Spread out, start combing all around," he shouted. It had registered that although the explosion came from a certain side, it didn't necessarily mean that the shot was also from that side. He contacted the helicopter overhead. The pilot could see him urgently pointing down the hill.

He contacted security at the gates. They assured him that the gates had just been closed and that the cemetery was now sealed off.

The subsequent inquiry into the killing was extremely critical of the three-minute delay before the gates were shut.

The bus driver had pulled in some twenty yards beyond the cemetery entrance and was standing at the front of his bus. The last passengers had just stepped down.

As soon as Dalton passed through the gates he strode purposefully over to the driver. "They want to talk to you," he said curtly.

He looked critically at the bus. "Move that a bit more out of the way. They'll want the road clear."

The driver obediently hopped back in.

Dalton climbed in beside him. Smoothly, he pressed the .38 into the man's side.

"Get moving and keep going over the bridge," he hissed.

The bus moved away from the cemetery.

When they had crossed back over the Potomac, Dalton ordered the driver to pull in along Twenty-third Street. The bemused and frightened man responded with alacrity. Dalton tossed the army cap onto a seat and told the man to lie facedown in the center aisle.

The high sides of the bus screened him as he knelt down, reversed the .38, and smashed it across the base of the man's skull. Still kneeling, he unbuttoned the army jacket, threw it on the ground, and stuffed the .38 under it. From now on it would only be a liability. He ripped off the long yellow stripes that he had tagged on the trousers, stood up from the unconscious driver, and hopped out of the bus. As he walked away, he looked like any other shirt-sleeved stroller.

Three minutes later he was at the underground parking lot where he had left the Pinto. The keys were still securely taped under the wheel arch. Half a minute later he was driving the Pinto up the front exit-ramp.

The lunchtime traffic was heavy. His destination was less than a mile away, but it took him over seven minutes to reach it. He parked in a quiet side street and removed the suitcase from the trunk. Hurrying back around the corner he entered the foyer of a large hotel. The hotel had been selected with his usual thoroughness. It was old and just on the right side of seedy.

He walked confidently through the lobby to the stairs and headed up. On the third floor he walked along the corridor until he found the only bathroom on that floor.

It was locked.

He returned to the stairs and headed up to the fourth floor. The bathroom here was vacant. He quickly locked himself in.

His body reeked of stale sweat. He removed all his clothes and spent two minutes methodically scrubbing himself under the hot shower. When he was dry, he opened the suitcase and began his preparations.

First he shaved himself very closely. He rubbed his hand along the skin. Rough to the touch, but the important thing was that it looked smooth.

When he was satisfied he started on his nails. The dirt was engrained under them, and climbing the tree had broken some of them. Using a pair of manicure scissors, he clipped them until all the jagged pieces were even. He then scrubbed them with a hard nail brush until they were thoroughly clean.

The next step was his eyes. He darkened the eyebrows with eyebrow pencil, applied some eye shadow, and pressed on the false eyelashes.

Next, the makeup on his cheeks and throat. He patted on a thick layer to cover any remaining stubble.

Red lipstick on the lips completed the transformation of his face.

He pulled a pair of tights up over his waist, fastened on a padded brassiere, and slipped a light green dress over his shoulders. The dress was full, and concealed the contours of his body. A silk scarf knotted around the throat covered his Adam's apple.

Flat, thin-soled sandals, fastened with white straps, made him seem even smaller.

He looked at himself in the mirror. If he found anything amusing in his appearance he didn't show it.

He removed the expensive wig from the suitcase. It had to be a good one. If a cheap wig was left rolled up in a polyethylene bag for long, it looked like a sod of wet turf. It was the wig which completed the transformation. The hair was thick and layered and cut in a distinctly feminine style. From the shaven oddity of a few seconds earlier, he could now easily pass as a woman.

The last attachments were the false fingernails. Not very long, but enough to alter the tips of his fingers from their somewhat squarish shape. A small handbag and a spray of Estée Lauder perfume completed the feminine picture.

From now on he must act and think like a woman. He had practiced the walk for hours, observing the walks of many different women until he felt he had it right. Sometimes a girl had seen him watching her and mistaken his interest for something else. Often he had been rewarded with a smile.

His voice was a problem. He had worked on that with a tape

recorder. A long conversation would finish him but he could maintain short bursts.

He stuffed his "male" clothes into the suitcase, left the bathroom, and walked along the corridor to the fire exit. Beside the exit was a wooden hatch containing a fire hose wrapped around a metal wheel. He quickly pressed the small suitcase into the space to the left of the wheel. It just fit in, standing upright in the space.

He walked back to the elevator and pressed the button. When it arrived, there were four people already in it. Three of them were men. After a brief glance they reverted to normal indifference. The doors closed and the elevator started to descend.

When it reached the lobby, Dalton walked straight out of the hotel. There was little resemblance between the short-haired young man who had entered the hotel twenty-five minutes earlier and the full-breasted young woman now leaving.

From the direction of the river he could hear the police sirens screeching their futile message. He hurried to his car.

As he drove northeast along New York Avenue, Dalton listened to the car radio. The announcer was excitedly relaying the news of the assassination. All scheduled programs had been cancelled. Road blocks were being put up all around Washington and travelers were requested to be as cooperative as possible with the police.

He met the first road block just beyond Brentwood Park. He pulled in behind the line of cars waiting to be checked. Every car was being stopped and its occupants closely questioned. His car edged to the front of the line.

He rolled down the window as the police officer approached. The officer looked through the window.

"Please step out of the car, ma'am."

Dalton swiveled his legs like a woman as he got out.

"May I see your license?"

Dalton fished the license out of the handbag and gave it to the policeman with what he hoped was a nice smile.

"Mrs. Leonora Davis?"

"Yes, officer," Dalton replied pleasantly.

"Where are you headed for, ma'am?" the officer asked.

"Philadelphia."

The photograph on the license obviously satisfied him as he returned it to Dalton after a brief glance.

"Please open the trunk, ma'am."

Dalton moved around to the back of the car in his best walk. The policeman gave the trunk a brief inspection.

"I'd like to look inside your car now."

"Certainly, officer. I heard the news on the radio about that British guy. My gawd, at Arlington . . . !" He tailed off, shaking his head as though at a loss for words.

Christ, supposing the wig fell off! He stopped shaking his head.

The policeman checked briefly under the seats.

"Thank you, ma'am. You can go through now."

Dalton smiled at him as he got back into the car.

He encountered two more road blocks within the next half hour but passed through without any problems.

He sped on toward New York.

• TWENTY-NINE •

ON THE NEW JERSEY TURNPIKE he was delayed by a multi-car pile-up. The light was just beginning to fade as he arrived in midtown Manhattan. He parked the car on Forty-sixth Street.

Entering a movie house on Broadway and Forty-seventh, he waited for half an hour. By then it was dark.

Outside again, he hailed a cab and ordered the cabbie to take him to the Federal Hall Memorial. He hoped that the guy wouldn't be too talkative. On arrival he paid the cabbie off and quickly walked down to the Staten Island Ferry. He purchased his ticket and hurried aboard. Twenty minutes later the engines started up and the ferry moved out into the harbor.

Dalton leaned on the rails and stared back at the illuminated Manhattan skyline. He didn't even see it. His mind was going over the events in the cemetery. Was it only this morning that it had all happened? Already it seemed so distant. Christ, he felt drained. Anyway, he'd soon be able to rest.

"Sure is beautiful, isn't it, honey?" said the man standing beside him.

Dalton looked sharply at him and then back at the skyline. He smiled weakly at the man. "Beautiful," he murmured before turning and walking away from the rail.

When the ferry gently bumped against the terminal pilings on the other side, he quickly disembarked. His destination was a large house about a mile from the terminal. He decided to risk a cab rather than walk. A lone woman pedestrian might be remembered.

He directed the cabbie to pull in three streets away from the house, and he walked the rest of the way. The house belonged to an elderly, childless couple who were sympathetic to the Movement, but not directly involved with it. The Leader had told him that the wife was a distant relative. The week before Dalton had arrived in

New York they had set off to enjoy a month-long holiday in Ireland. All they knew was that their house would be required for a short period. They didn't ask any questions.

Like the other houses on the avenue, this house was detached and set well back from the road. The ivy clinging to its walls enhanced its air of solid respectability, and leafy trees insured the privacy of the occupants.

Dalton walked up the graveled drive and located the key under a stone. He let himself into the house and walked down to the basement before switching on the light. From the outside, the light would not be visible. The basement was fully furnished and had a color TV. On the sofa were two packages.

Dalton longed to stretch out immediately, but first he had to wash the makeup off his face. He returned upstairs to the bathroom, stripped naked, and showered in the dark. When he had finished he padded back down to the basement, still dripping wet.

He opened the packages. Besides a selection of fresh clothes, one of them contained a gun and ammunition. Another .38. If all went well he wouldn't need to use the gun. The owner of the house had acquired it some months previously. As a matter of course, all identification had been filed off.

Dalton dried himself and stretched out naked on the bed. This would be his home for the next five days. The refrigerator was well-stocked, and he noted gratefully that there seemed to be plenty of reading material about. It would be a long wait.

No matter how hard they looked he was safe here. On the night of the fifth day, he would make his way to a jetty on the Hudson River. There he would board a Canadian cargo ship registered out of Saint John. The captain of the ship was Canadian-born, but of Irish parents. He had been brought up in their strict Republican tradition. Nobody else on the ship would know of Dalton's presence.

The captain would meet him at a warehouse on the wharf and Dalton would be concealed in a large wooden crate. The crate would have plenty of air vents and a supply of food and water. This crate would be one of the last to be hoisted aboard. Once it was aboard, the ship would set sail almost immediately. The route to Canada was one that the ship traveled frequently and the captain was well-known to the harbor-masters.

Dalton was realistic enough to know that after the assassination no country on earth would be safe for him. His success would condemn him to a life as a fugitive. He had talked it out with the Leader before the final decision. He knew that he would be exempt from any amnesty that might follow. No matter what happened, the British and Americans would always want to extradite him. It was likely that he would be a wanted man for the rest of his life. He had chosen the path he would travel himself.

The Leader would provide for him. After arrival in Canada, he would be hidden there for a month. The only person involved would be the cargo captain. The hunt for the killer would still be intense but it would have lost some of its initial thrust.

The captain would handle the arrangements to ship him to Argentina. After a short interval he would undergo radical plastic surgery, including fingerprint obliteration. A well-guarded farm would provide him with plenty of security. Money would be no problem, even if he had to stay in South America forever.

As he drifted into sleep his thoughts were on Argentina. . . .

He woke instantly.

Total darkness.

He slipped out of the bed and into the trousers and shoes. The noise had come from outside.

He moved silently up the stairs, pulling on his shirt as he moved. The .38 was in his right hand.

He had just reached the top of the stairs when the searchlights lit up the front of the house. The sudden brightness was dazzling. Luckily he hadn't yet reached a window.

He dived on the floor and crawled through the hall toward the back of the house.

Also lit up.

He heard his name being called through a loudspeaker at the front and crawled back out there again.

The words were clear.

"Surrounded . . . no escape . . . hands on head. Surrender peacefully."

He sat with his back against the wall. He knew then.

His decision had been made a long time ago. The prospect of

spending the rest of his life in an American jail was no more acceptable than its equivalent in England. He had chosen the path of his own life, and now he would choose how he died.

Sliding under the window sill to the front door, he paused there for a few seconds. He was ready now.

He jerked the door open and came out firing.

Fleeting shadows. Three blinding searchlights. One of his shots knocked out a light but it was only a gesture. The remaining searchlights pinned him for the police marksmen.

Dalton's life ended.

• THIRTY •

THE MAN COMPLETED THE PHONE CALL.
  The ashtray was full again. He sighed and emptied the cigar butts into the open fire.
  There was no other way.
  It was vital that the British were not sidetracked. The focus of attention must be centered on the horror of the Prime Minister's assassination and, indirectly, the reason for that killing. A long hunt for the killer would only divert attention from the important issues.
  Likewise, the Americans must not be diverted. They would take it as a terrible blow to their prestige if the assassin managed to escape. It was bad enough that the Prime Minister had been assassinated on American soil; bad enough that they knew an attempt was planned and had a description of the killer. But that the killer could completely elude them and get away scot-free was unthinkable. American politicians would have to be very careful about their utterances on Ireland in the future. Any criticism of British policy would provoke the unanswerable retort that a country which had allowed their Prime Minister to be killed, and had not even apprehended the killer, had no right to give them advice.
  At the time that he had made his phone call, the police and FBI were being scorched by media and politicians alike. The information that the anonymous caller had given to the American Embassy in Dublin had been explicit. There was absolutely no doubt that the caller knew all the details of the assassination. He had finished by telling them that the killer would not surrender under any circumstances.
  The attention that he and Dalton had given to the escape to South America had been just as meticulous as the rest of the plan. He had too much respect for Dalton to propose anything that wasn't entirely feasible.

If Dalton had somehow evaded the police in the house, there would have been no ship to take him to Canada, no organization to help him.

He could not be given a chance. The house would be his tomb as soon as he entered it. It was important that he was not taken alive. A long trial would also divert attention.

Already the uncritical and extravagantly phrased eulogies for the Prime Minister were filling the papers. The real assessments that would herald the changes would come later. . . .

R0142277805 HUM

HOUSTON PUBLIC LIBRARY

CENTRAL LIBRARY
500 MCKINNEY

MAY   1981